BETWEEN A WITCH AND A HARD PLACE

Vanessa Kinley, Witch PI, Book 1

CELIA ROMAN

BONE DIGGERS PRESS
www.bonediggerspress.com

For Levi
who wields his own brand of magic

First edition © 2022 C.D. Watson. All Rights Reserved.
Cover design © Nocturne Art.
Published by Bone Diggers Press, Clayton, Georgia.
ISBN 978-1-943465-68-2

10 9 8 7 6 5 4 3 2 1

ONE

I live by three nevers.

Never pick a fight I can't win.

Never date a guy with hair prettier than mine.

And never, ever, under any circumstance, have anything to do with a vampire.

Call them rules, call them guidelines, call them whatever the hell you want, but whenever I violate one of those nevers, something bad is sure to follow.

So when a vampire planted himself next to me at Kinley's, my brother's bar, I took one look at the lush black waves of hair brushing the collar of his shirt and said, "Nope."

Mr. Tall, Dark, and Sexy arched a perfect black eyebrow at me. "I didn't ask a question."

The faint hint of an accent underscored his words, making them seem more like sex dipped in chocolate than communication.

I stifled the automatic thrill running down my spine. Vampires had that effect on everyone. No need to take it personally.

"You were about to," I said. "And I said no."

Nick, my brother and the owner of Kinley's, winked at me over the wooden bar running the length of the back wall. He was working tonight, his black Kinley's t-shirt stretching tight over lean muscle as he mixed drinks. He and I were twins, fraternal, and as unlike each other as night and day. He was tall, blonde, and muscled, and ladies flocked to him like flies to honey.

I, on the other hand, was short and dumpy with mousy hair I'd started dying at the grand old age of sixteen, when our mom up and abandoned us to the mean suburban streets of Crossville, Georgia, a bedroom community of Atlanta.

As for my ability to attract men, that's where Nevers Two and Three came in.

Behind Nick, a mirror reflected Kinley's patronage between the bottles of wine and liquor displayed on glass shelves in front of it. There my short self was, the pink bob of my hair framing a pale face above the black t-shirt emblazoned with the bar's hot pink logo.

And there was the space beside me, completely empty of Mr. Tall, Dark, and Reflectionless.

Yup. Definitely a vampire.

I sighed as I glanced at that empty mirror again, then at the vamp's smooth, handsome features and the lithe sexiness hidden beneath a long-sleeved black shirt and jeans. Damn shame about those rules.

Nick must've caught my sigh. He placed the last of the mixed drinks Table 6 had ordered on my tray and grinned. "Just 'cause he's a vamp, Nessie," he said, pitching his voice over the usual Friday night noise where everyone nearby, including the vamp, could hear.

On cue, my cheeks suffused with hot heat. "Thanks, Nicky. With brothers like you, who needs enemies?"

The vamp in question leaned perfectly muscled forearms against the bar, putting his head half a foot above mine. "I need you," he said.

His quiet statement did all sorts of funny things to my stomach, but I barked out a short laugh as I hefted the drink-laden tray and turned. "Sure, you do, pal."

His eyebrows furrowed into a frown, marring the smooth, marble-white skin of his forehead.

My own forehead would grow wrinkles if I did that.

With a brisk shake of my head, I wove through the crowd toward Table 6. It wasn't too bad tonight. Mostly thirty- and forty-somethings watching the football game playing on a widescreen in one corner, conveniently angled toward the bar. A few older folks sat at the bar proper, watching the game or nursing a longneck, and the occasional supernatural slid easily through the crowd, their differences unnoticed by the humans.

Supes were good at blending in. And most humans were clueless, even when the supes *didn't* blend so well.

It was a good crowd. A *happy* crowd, even for a Friday, and that's exactly the kind of crowd I liked. Happy customers tipped better, for one, and for another, they were less likely to start fights or grope my rear.

I dropped the drinks off at Table 6, chitchatted for half a minute with the two men and one woman sitting there, then tucked the tray under my arm and checked the rest of my section. I was responsible for about one-third of the floor tonight, which would've been nearly the entire bar just six months ago.

Since then, Nick had expanded into an adjoining space and added a small stage, a slightly larger dance floor, and more tables. He'd hired a rotating crew of part-time servers to cover the new area and part of the old bar, leaving two four-tops and four booths for his regular Friday night server to cover.

For whom I was filling in. I had my own job, thank you very much, but when Nick needed me to lend a hand, I did. Like tonight, which had naturally put me on a headlong course with a vamp.

I turned away from a male supe of indeterminate origins sitting alone at Table 2 and the half dozen post-shift nurses squeezed into Table 3, and ran headlong into said vamp's chest.

His hands caught my arms, steadying me, and I looked way up, completely forgetting to avoid his mesmerizing gaze.

"I need you," he repeated, his soft, sensual voice weaving a spell around me.

His eyes were black and oh, so tempting. If I were fully human, they would draw me in, bespell me, leaving me vulnerable to his deepest desire. The witch in me, small though it was, provided some resistance to a vampire's mesmer.

Not enough, apparently. I felt myself melt against him as my skin flushed and my heart kicked up a notch.

His mouth curled into a grin. "Not that way, though I'm happy to oblige."

"Er." I shook my head, clearing it a little, and refocused my gaze on his throat as I pushed away from him. It didn't help. His hands were oddly warm against my skin and his right thumb was stroking my left bicep, inciting some mighty interesting heat in places I'd rather not think about with a blood-sucking vamp inches away from me. "What did you need again?"

"It's about your mother. Is there somewhere we can talk?"

Anger hit me so hard, I would've swayed if the vampire hadn't had a good hold on my arms. I didn't want to talk about her. At all. Why should I? She *left* me and Nick and...

My gaze drifted to my brother where he stood behind the bar, building a Guinness for a regular. His eyes shone bright and he was laughing, but twelve years ago, just after our sixteenth birthday when Mom walked out, he'd been a devastated wreck. I couldn't help him then, but maybe I could help him now, by making sure that woman never had a chance to hurt him again.

Even if it meant talking to a vampire.

I shook my head again, keeping my gaze down around his neck. "I'm off at midnight. We can talk then."

He nodded tightly and let me go, and I walked back to the bar on legs turned to jelly by a simple touch.

Unfortunately for me, the vamp chose to park himself at the bar for the remaining three hours of my shift, a bold move considering his obvious lack of a reflection. Nick served him a water with a slice of lime twisted onto the rim. Danged if the vamp didn't sip it while watching the succession of games playing on the TV.

Apparently, he was a fan.

And just as apparently, he wasn't paying me a bit of attention.

I wished I could say the same. Wherever I went, the back of my neck prickled as if someone were watching me, even when I bounced into the kitchen to pick up an order. The reaction of prey to a predator. When I looked, though, the vamp's gaze was always elsewhere.

My hyper awareness of Mr. Tall, Dark, and Deadly combined with the lingering anger over Mom made time seem as if it had come to a standstill. By the time midnight rolled around, I was beat and ready for a hot shower, a good book, and the cushy comfort of my king-sized bed.

At precisely midnight, though, the vampire rose from his barstool, paid his tab, and settled his gaze on me as if I were din-din.

Which I wasn't. *Ever.* Going. To be.

I did a final sweep of my station, making sure everyone was settled, then let one of the new servers know I was leaving, cashed out my apron, and clocked out.

And finally, I couldn't put it off any longer.

With a deep breath, I snagged my keys from Nick's desk, made my way from the back rooms to the bar proper, and found the vamp. "Ok," I told him. "We can go to my office."

Without waiting for an acknowledgment, I pivoted on a very tired heel and marched toward the front door. Somehow, he was there ahead of me, holding it open from the inside, leaving me precious little room to pass.

I brushed by him without giving my uneasiness away, I hoped, and headed around the corner to my own office, separated from Kinley's by the narrow stairway leading to the apartments that Nick and I rented, located above the bar.

Seeing my office door always gave me a small thrill. I'd had it painted in gold and black lettering the moment I'd gotten my business license, about five minutes after quitting the Crossville PD where I'd been one of two detectives.

Vanessa Kinley, the door read. *Private Investigator.*

Yeah, that's me. The big P.I.

With a smile, I inserted the key into the lock, twisted it open, and led Mr. Sexy Blood Sucker into the receptionist's area.

Or what would be the receptionist's area when I hired an actual receptionist.

The tiny room held a small desk situated to the right of the door leading into my office. A potted plant and two leather-and-wood chairs set against the wall to the right of the entryway filled the rest of the space. The indoor-outdoor carpeting was dark gray and perfectly offset the eggshell-colored walls. A collection of framed certificates from my days with the PD hung on the far right wall right next to my college diploma.

It would do, I decided, and flipped on the light.

The vamp apparently thought it would do, too, since he closed the door and settled into one of the chairs facing the desk.

Damned if I'd take the other one. Instead, I leaned my rear against the as yet unhired receptionist's desk and crossed my arms over my chest. "Ok, Mister...?"

"Dimitri Stanislov, at your service."

I only just refrained from rolling my eyes. Of course, he was. That name explained the accent and the manners. Old world vamps. Gotta love 'em.

"What about Mom dragged you out to the 'burbs to talk to me, Mr. Stanislov?"

Dimitri relaxed into the chair, his expression bland. "Galena is missing, Miss Kinley, and I need you to find her."

TWO

I managed to keep my jaw from gaping only because my anger kicked back into gear. This vampire wanted me to find the woman who'd abandoned me and Nick the minute she got tired of us?

Who the hell did he think he was?

If my anger showed, Dimitri didn't react. I swallowed it down, tried to force my tense muscles to relax, and failed.

Oh, well. Work with what you've got.

"What makes you think I want to find her?" I said.

To his credit, Stanislov appeared to give my question due consideration. "She's your mother. Is that not enough of a reason?"

"No. And if I'd known that's what you wanted before I brought you here, I would've said no then, too."

"What did you expect me to say?"

Anything but that. Honestly, anything. Her being dead ranked a lot higher on my internal list of things he wanted to talk about than her being missing. And the thought of her being dead hadn't even stirred a care.

"I'm not interested." My voice was tight and thin, my mouth

a little numb. "Which I'm sure you knew before you waltzed into my brother's bar."

To his credit, Dimitri nodded once, regally. "If the situation were not dire—"

I barked out a laugh, cut it off when tears threatened to well up. Damn it. I thought I'd conquered this a long time ago. *Years* ago. It had taken so much effort to get to a point where the mere mention of that woman didn't set off an emotional reaction outside of anger, where I didn't resent merely hearing her name.

I swallowed down the emotion and tried again.

"Let's be clear," I said. "My mother walked out in the middle of the night, leaving me and Nick to fend for ourselves. We woke up the next morning to find her gone. No note, not a single goddamned word of warning. She just disappeared. And now you want me to find her?"

"If you would allow me to explain, Miss Kinley."

"Forget it." I pushed off the desk, strode across the room, and opened the door, letting in the cool, late summer air. "Get out. Now."

Dimitri rose and turned toward me. "Galena is your mother. Have you no care?"

Hysterical laughter bubbled up again, and was ruthlessly tamped down. "She stopped being my mother the day she abandoned me."

"Then you will not help me?"

I jiggled the door again, truly angry now. "How many ways do I have to say no?"

"You will contact me when you change your mind."

"Not likely, pal."

He nodded again and glided forward, then stopped directly in front of me. I looked way up, intending to dress him down. Would've, too, if not for his vampiric reflexes. So quickly I had zero time to react, he grabbed my wrist and raised it to his mouth. Before I could yank it away, his fangs scored the flesh of my inner wrist.

Blood welled up and my breath caught in my throat.

"What the hell!" I muttered as he scored his own wrist's flesh and pressed the two wounds together.

"Blood to blood," he said. "You will contact me when you change your mind. Goodnight, Miss Kinley."

He was gone before I could do more than blink into the slight wind his departure generated.

My anger deflated like a stuck balloon and fatigue washed over me. I looked down at my wrist, at the already coagulating blood gathering on top of the skin. The wound was small, just big enough to bleed, and it tingled gently.

Not good. Damn it.

I closed the door and locked it, then headed toward the bathroom nestled into the back beyond my office. A good scrubbing, some antibiotic cream, and a band-aid should do the trick. Then I was by golly going home and taking a long, hot bath with a good book and a bottle of Nick's finest red as my companions.

Nick knocked on the bathroom door half an hour later. I'd just gotten into the tub with my book and wine, and now, I was glad I'd left my apartment door unlocked for him.

What the hell. We were the only two people with access to this side of the second story. Except the landlord, and he never bothered checking on us.

I swallowed the tiny bite of dark chocolate I'd bitten off, sank low enough for the thick layer of bubbles to cover the important parts, and hollered, "Come in."

Nick opened the door and stuck his head in, scowling. "You shouldn't leave your front door unlocked. What if somebody snuck up here from the bar?"

"I would've shot them."

Did I mention the Glock I'd dropped into a holster nailed to the wall beside the tub? Color me paranoid, but I tried to be prepared.

Nick's expression cleared and he stepped into the

bathroom. "Once a big brother."

"A seven-minute age difference doesn't count."

"Does, too."

He closed the toilet's lid and sat down facing me, his hands loose between his knees. The old joke had eased some of the worry, but not all of it. There was a slight pinch between his thick, blonde eyebrows that hadn't been there earlier.

"What'd the vamp want?" he said.

Ah. That's where the worry came from. I marked my spot in the book I was reading (a trashy romance, thanks much) and handed it to him, waiting until he put it on the sink's lip before speaking.

"He wanted to hire me." I shifted uneasily in the water and sighed. There was no easy way to put this, but I sure as hell wasn't hiding it from him. "He said Mom has gone missing and he wants me to find her."

Nick's gaze went vacant, and his lips pressed together into a thin slash. "What did you tell him?"

"To get lost."

"Hmm."

"Hmm what?"

He sat there thinking for a minute while the water cooled. Music from the bar filled the silence, a dim thump of strong bass and country twang. On the street below, a car drove by, its muffler jarringly loud, and the wind gusted once, rattling the shutters outside the bathroom's lone window.

Finally, Nick's gaze lowered to mine and he held out a hand. I lifted mine out of the water and touched his fingers, and a familiar connection zinged between us. The love of two people who'd shared a womb. The friendship we'd forged when we were kids, united against the headstrong power of a woman we'd later learned was a witch. And the faint tingle of our own shared power, a magic we'd never used together in the dozen years since learning what we were.

Nick's fingers tightened on mine. "I think you should do it."

My jaw dropped for half a second before I snapped it shut.

"Find Mom? Are you serious?"

"Yeah. What if she's hurt?"

He'd never given up hope. Damn it. I shoved down the automatic surge of protective anger. Nick had been a lot closer to Mom than me. Her leaving like she did had hurt me, but Nick? It had taken him years to recover.

"She's a big girl, Nicky," I said, as gently as I could manage. "Whatever she's gotten herself into, she can get herself out of."

"No, I..." His gaze went vacant again and he shook his head. "I have a funny feeling about this."

"That feeling is indigestion. It's what happens when you eat your own cooking."

He laughed and let my hand slip out of his. "With sisters like you—"

"Who needs enemies. Yeah, yeah." I waved a hand at my book and took it from him when he retrieved it from the sink, then pointed to the door. "Get back to work. I've got a book to read and a glass of wine to enjoy."

"Slave driver," he said, grinning.

"That's me, the driver o' slaves named Nick Kinley."

He slipped out the door chuckling, but the conversation had left me unsettled.

What if Mom was hurt? What if, as Nick suggested, she needed some help getting out of whatever trouble she'd landed in?

More importantly, why did we have to be the someones getting her out of said trouble? She'd abandoned us, just left, and she hadn't bothered to come back or contact us or any of the things a remorseful person would do. What did we owe her after all this time?

I turned back to my book and the wine, attempting to relax, but the doubts bouncing around in my head distracted me until well after bedtime.

THREE

I slept late the next morning and woke groggy and grumpy, with the faint hint of a bad dream lingering around the edges of my consciousness. Something about Nick and me, when we were young. We'd done something terribly wrong. All I could really remember was the terror on Mom's face, which morphed into a formless thundercloud spewing lightning through a dense rain.

I shook off the dream's vestiges, slapped around the nightstand for my cellphone, and checked my text messages. That was a bad habit from my days on the force, one I'd never been able to break.

Today I had a text from Auntie O waiting for me. Ophelia, an unrelated friend of the family, had taken me and Nick in when Mom disappeared. She'd advised us not to contact the police, and not long after, we'd learned why. Dear ol' Mom was a witch, and a powerful one at that.

Nick and I, as hereditary witches, would've been in dire trouble if we'd been placed in a human foster home. Something about witch politics and Mom's place in the supernatural community, Auntie said, though Nick and I had never been aware of any of that before then.

Long story short, we were better off with her, even if she'd never been able to coax more than a trickle of magic out of either one of us. I'd managed to learn one spell based on a simple rune, just one. Nick hadn't even managed that.

Auntie O was a gifted diviner. She'd hoped to pass her knowledge on to one of us, since she had no children of her own. Alas. Neither of us possessed the talent for it.

I thumbed into Auntie's text, expecting a customary *just checking on my godchildren* text. Instead, her message read, *Beware of men with pointy teeth.*

My mind leapt immediately to the vampire and the case he'd wanted me to take, probably without pay. Or, at least, I assumed he wasn't going to pay me for it.

Pay me to find my own mother.

I grunted and set my phone down. That warning had come a few hours too late. Auntie must be slipping in her old age.

Normally, I liked to wallow in the luxury of Egyptian cotton sheets on my mornings off, but this morning, I knew better. If I stayed here, with my body inactive and my mind free to wander, I'd worry myself to death over the vampire's visit.

With a sigh, I dragged myself out of bed, went potty and brushed my teeth, then pulled on cutoff sweats and a ragged t-shirt and put the treadmill wedged into one corner of my living room to good use.

Forty minutes later, my skin was flushed and slick with sweat and my legs felt like rubber, but my mind was clear. I texted Nick to see if he wanted to grab lunch and showered while waiting for a reply. One hadn't popped up by the time I finished dressing. Probably still asleep. Weekends were hard on him, poor baby.

But that's what he got for owning a bar.

I, on the other hand, had regular business hours, eight to five on weekdays. Of course, I usually ended up working weird hours when I was on a case. Cheating spouses were just rude that way, always sneaking into hotels for cheap sex in the middle of the night when they thought no one would notice.

Little did they know.

I walked downstairs in a slightly better mood, even enduring the miserably rainy day without complaint as I unlocked my office and slipped inside. The bar opened at eleven on Saturdays, but Nick usually worked the late shift, when the bigger crowds came in to catch a game with friends, listen to the weekend's band, or take a turn on the dance floor. Music drifted to me, quieter during the lunch rush than it'd been last night. By the time Nick poked his head into my office an hour later, my toes were tapping and my grumpies were gone.

"Hey," he said. "You look like crap."

"Thanks, brother dear." I closed the folder I was working on, a fraud investigation for a local insurance company, and dropped it onto my active cases pile. "You look gloriously handsome as ever."

I'd said it to needle him, but it was true. Nick woke up looking like he'd stepped out of GQ. The real reason I was pissed at Mom? She gave him all the good genes.

Nick grinned at me and propped a muscular shoulder against the doorframe. "Still covering for Wanda tonight?"

"You betcha!" I put enough fake chipper into my voice to make him wince. "I so look forward to meager tips, sore feet, and getting my butt grabbed by drunks and scoundrels."

"Hey, now. Kinley's is too classy for scoundrels."

"Are you kidding? Scoundrels are the best part. If nothing else, they're good for practicing my Jiu-Jitsu."

"I should make you the bouncer," he said dryly. "So. About lunch."

"Did anyone ever tell you you're a slave to your stomach?"

"Just my stomach."

I laughed and grabbed my wallet, a flat leather folding rectangle just big enough to hold my debit card, an emergency credit card, and some cash. Conveniently enough, it fit into the inside pocket of the leather jacket I wore at this time of year, when summer's heat gave way to fall's milder temperatures.

Just as I was grabbing my phone and searching for an umbrella, someone knocked on the outer door.

Nick arched his eyebrows at me as he pushed off the doorframe. "Expecting someone?"

"No, not on a Saturday."

Except Mr. Pointy Teeth, maybe. If the knocker was him, I'd be more than happy to tell him no again. Outside, where he might be exposed to the sun, if it ever stopped raining. Which should be interesting, given the whole *vampires are allergic to sunlight* thing.

I stuck my phone in the back pocket of my jeans, tucked my wallet away, and headed toward the door, the umbrella forgotten. The shadow looming through the frosted glass was entirely too bulky to be my would-be client from last night.

I flipped the lock and pulled the door open, then sighed. Our landlord stood there, scowling down from a height a good foot above the top of my vertically challenged head. Seth owned many of the buildings along this street, from Kinley's at the corner of Winfield and Main all the way down Winfield to Buncombe Avenue. He was the alpha of the local werewolf pack, which made him a Mr. Pointy Teeth of a different and just as deadly kind. Thankfully, we only had to worry about that sort of thing on the full moon.

Anyway, it was prime real estate, but the rent was cheap, mostly due to a friend of a supernatural friend kinda thing. Seth gave priority to supernaturals when he rented, especially werewolves. Which Nick and I were not, but apparently witches were ok, too, even half witches.

In return for a prime location and a good deal on the rent, Nick provided a sanctuary of sorts for the local supes, including members of Seth's pack.

My contribution to the reduced rent had once been acting as the unofficial liaison between Seth and the Crossville Police Department. Now, I provided investigative services when Seth needed them, which wasn't often. Seth's lieutenants had good noses for ferreting out that sort of thing, and I meant that literally.

I smiled up at him, too used to his perpetual *weight of the world on my broad shoulders* demeanor to be intimidated by his scowl. Though I still hadn't quite forgiven him for ruining the one and only date I'd had this year.

"Hey, Seth," I said. "Did we forget to pay the rent?"

He did a double take, which was kinda funny. Seth was built like a rock wall, all hard angles and strength, and had the intestinal fortitude to match. He didn't rattle easily. "Miles didn't say anything."

Miles being the lieutenant in charge of the pack's finances. Seth wasn't a mob boss, but he did run his financials like one, minus the baseball bat to the knees thing. That wasn't necessary. Seth, as the one of the most powerful supernaturals around, scared humans on a level so deep, most intuitively knew better than to mess with him even when they didn't know what he was. As for the rest of the creatures living in Crossville, only a stupid supe picked a fight with an alpha.

Miles had the same effect, though he barely topped five eight, wore glasses, and was slender as a reed. He looked more like the accountant he'd been before the Change than Seth's collector, but I wasn't fooled by his mild manners. Werewolves were freakishly strong and had reflexes on par with a vampire's. Plus, their sensitive noses could pick up scents from miles away. Once they got a good whiff of you, they could track you down with fear-inducing speed.

It was what they did to you for running that put the fear of God into other supes.

Nick and I didn't worry about that because, like good little half witches with virtually no magic to speak of, we paid the rent on time. There's power in responsibility.

"I'm teasing," I said, and stepped back, giving Seth room to enter. I closed the door behind him as he and Nick shook hands and exchanged greetings. "We need to work on that."

Seth's scowl reappeared. "Work on what?"

"Teasing," I said gently. "It's not like you to lose track of a conversation."

His nostrils flared. "I smell vampire."

"Client."

He leaned down close enough for me to see the gold flecks in his eyes. "In your blood."

My cheeks heated and I stepped hastily back. Damn vampire. That little cut on my wrist hadn't scabbed over yet and it itched, too. If I ever saw Dimitri again, I'd be sure to give him an earful about stealing blood when you weren't invited to it.

"What brings you by, Seth?" I said.

Thankfully, he straightened and let the vampire thing go. I didn't know what I would've done if he'd pressed the matter. Vampires and werewolves don't exactly mix well, and Seth knew I'd sworn off vampires.

"We've had some..." The hard line of his mouth twisted into a frown. "Trouble."

"What kind of trouble?"

"A female went missing."

Goose bumps crawled down my spine and I shivered. "Whose mate?"

"Unmated. A natural born wolf."

Seth raked both hands through his slightly damp, chestnut brown hair and threaded his fingers together on top of his head. His biceps bulged underneath the tight t-shirt he wore, and I tried not to fangirl. The wolf was *built.*

"A junior at Crossville Community College," he added.'

Too old for teenage hijinks then. Crossville was a picture of Suburbia, but we still had the occasional teen runaway.

"Walk me through what you know," I said.

Seth nodded and dropped his hands. "Sure. It won't take long."

Nick walked over and squeezed my shoulder. "How about I grab some lunch from the kitchen and bring it over for y'all?"

I nodded and turned to Seth, who said yes, then Nick left, and Seth and I went back to my office to talk.

* * *

The young wolf's name was Serena Jimenez. Latina, brown/brown, five five in her socks, with a tiny birthmark near the left corner of her mouth. Her father, a nail driver, was a mid-level wolf in Seth's pack and her mother had died giving birth to Serena's baby sister.

Tragic, but not uncommon in werewolf-human matings.

Serena had been seven at the time, and she'd taken her duties as the elder sister seriously, helping her father with the new baby whenever she could. The family was close-knit and active in the wolf and human communities. Members of St. Mary's, a Catholic church on the other side of the downtown area. Like many other local werewolves, the family participated in recreational sports leagues. Serena volunteered as a mentor and tutor at her sister's school, around holding two part-time jobs, being a full-time student, and playing intramural soccer at Crossville Community College where she was studying business.

I let out a huff of air when Seth wound up his summary of her life. "Sheesh. When did she have time to breathe?"

The hard slash of his mouth didn't even twitch toward a smile. "She's a go-getter. A lot of wolf females are."

I pressed my lips together, holding in a retort. Being a go-getter was probably the only way Serena could compete. Female wolves were strong, but nowhere near on par with their male counterparts.

Plus, pack politics could be...patriarchal. Seth was one of the more open-minded alphas. He even had a female lieutenant, a tough as nails she-wolf named Mariah who served as his enforcer.

Yeah, a female enforcer. But it worked for them, so not a soul complained. Those who did tended to end up with mysterious wounds that took a long, long time to heal.

"When did Serena go missing?" I said.

"Yesterday evening, around six thirty." Seth leaned back in the chair. It creaked dangerously under his weight, and I made a mental note to buy sturdier chairs as soon as my meager budget allowed. "She was coming home from a late class. The last

Horatio heard—"

"Horatio?"

"Her father. The last text he got from her said that she was stuck in a drive-thru, waiting to order supper for the family."

I asked which restaurant and wrote down Seth's gruff response, then jotted a note to get a copy of the text thread from Mr. Jimenez so I could follow up with the restaurant. If she'd made it through the drive-thru, chances were good someone had seen her. Maybe the restaurant had her on film. That would firm up the timeline.

"How far is it from there to home? Wait, does she still live at home, or does she live in a dorm?"

"Home. Her sister's young still."

I nodded. Single dad, kid sister. Yeah, they needed the extra help.

"Do you want the time between the restaurant and their house at the speed limit or the flow of traffic?"

"There's a difference?" I shook my head. Of course, he would know both times. He'd probably already driven the likely routes a few times each and timed every run. "On average."

"Twelve minutes with normal traffic."

He rattled off the Jimenez's home address, and I jotted it down, then murmured, "I'll need to go drive that."

Seth stood abruptly. "Ok. We can take my car."

The look I shot him must've been as startled as I felt. He sat down and glowered at me. "Or you can drive, and I can take shotgun."

"We're eating lunch first," I said firmly. "Because you're a werewolf, you burn a lot of calories, and I can hear your stomach growling from here."

He put a protective hand over his flat stomach. "Sorry. Long day."

"I was teasing." Again. Tough crowd. "I'm hungry. So we eat while I pry more information out of you, and then we can go drive the route."

"Routes. She's a wolf."

And werewolves are paranoid security freaks. Serena would've had multiple ways home and varied her routes at random. It made it easy to spot and evade a tail, something her father would've taught her to do before she learned to drive. Female werewolves weren't exactly rare, but they weren't exactly common either, especially hereditary wolves. Rogues targeted them from time to time in a desperate bid for a mate and the security of a pack, and occasionally, they were targeted for other reasons, just like any other female.

Serena would've been tough, though. She sounded tough anyway, and Seth made sure the females in his pack knew how to handle themselves.

Which begged the question as to what had happened to her. If Serena was as devoted to her family as Seth made out, she wouldn't have left them high and dry. She could've had an accident, sure, but Crossville wasn't that big. Someone would've spotted her vehicle and called for help, which would've alerted the pack almost immediately.

Had she gone off course somehow, for some unknown reason? Boyfriend? Friend friends? Party night? What would've tempted her to not drive straight home, relatively speaking?

I didn't want to beg trouble, but I knew that if I ruled all that out, that left kidnapping. Seth had probably already thought of it. He was sharp as a tack behind those roughly chiseled features, a lack of appreciation for gentle teasing notwithstanding. But I wasn't going to bring it up until I'd ruled out everything else.

The front door opened, and Nick hollered, letting us know it was him. Seth was already standing. I bet he'd smelled the food as soon as Nick had walked out of Kinley's with it, even though the bar's front entrance was around the corner on Main.

I shook my head and cleared off my desk, my mind already working the angles.

FOUR

The restaurant from which Serena had texted her father was a local burger chain on the south side of town, off the Atlanta Highway. It was a rectangular box of a store with bright red trim and plate glass windows fronting the customer side.

The light rain I'd walked through before lunch had turned to a miserable drizzle as the afternoon wore on. Now, the sun sat halfway between its zenith and the horizon, taking much of its light and heat with it, and streetlights had started popping on. We were maybe two hours from sunset, and already, I was glad for my jacket.

Mariah, Seth's enforcer, was waiting in the parking lot for me and Seth to arrive. She was five ten if she was an inch and sturdy. Not muscled or fat, just tough. The most remarkable thing about her, outside of her attitude, was her copper-colored hair. It fell in a long, straight sheet down past her shoulder blades, a perfect foil for her whiskey brown eyes and skin a shade darker.

All three were natural, courtesy of a mixed heritage Mariah didn't talk about much. Or ever. Played her cards close to her chest, did that one.

It's not that we didn't get along so much as that Mariah didn't particularly care for anyone, especially anyones of a female persuasion, and particularly females attached to Seth.

Seth and I had never been anything more than friends, and that mostly because of his friendship with Nick. Apparently that was close enough. Mariah gave me the stink eye every time she saw me. It would've worn me down if it weren't so unnecessary. I had no designs on Seth, though I could appreciate her protective instincts.

She jerked a chin at me when we approached, then turned to Seth. Today she wore an olive-green explorer jacket over a black tank-top and jeans that fit just right, an outfit I could never pull off because *curves*.

On the other hand, I had a better waist indent than her, so take that, Amazon wolf.

She and Seth were doing that silent wolf communication thing, sharing feelings and thoughts through some quasi-telepathic bond. I cleared my throat to remind them that I, a lowly witch-human hybrid, needed actual spoken words, and Mariah turned her flat stare on me.

"Nothing," she said, her voice a rich, smooth contralto. "No Serena smells."

"Serena smells?" I said.

"Shampoo, soap, perfume, laundry detergent, nail polish, car exhaust—"

"Ok, I get it."

And wondered why I'd bothered asking. *Of course*, Mariah had a complete catalog of Serena's smells in her head. That was who she was.

She turned back to Seth, her arms loose at her sides. "I caught a whiff of magic."

"What kind?" he said.

She shook her head once, and her hair shimmered along her shoulders. "Weird scent, like every magic, but none on its own."

The hairs on the back of my neck prickled. I wiped a hand

my nape, trying to rub out the unease.

Every magic, but none on its own.

Sounded like chaos magic. Or, no, that wasn't the right way to put it. A chaos witch could draw on magic through multiple forms of ritual and whatnot. The magic itself was not exactly formless, but not so distinctive that it could easily be labeled. *Oh, that's kitchen magic and that's garden magic.* No, nothing like that. The magic simply existed. How we drew on it, how we directed it; that was where labels came in.

Most witches mastered one to three different methods, depending on so many factors it was impossible to list all of them. But a chaos witch could, with practice, tap effortlessly into magic using whatever tool was at hand or, depending on the witch, no tool at all, making them one of the more rare practitioners.

While I wasn't acquainted with every local witch, I knew a lot of them, either through Auntie O or from my days with the Crossville PD. I knew of only one chaos witch, though. They were that rare.

Seth turned a flat stare on me. "What?"

"Nothing." Not nothing, but not something either. I had no idea how to explain witchcraft to him beyond what he already knew. Chances were, he knew more than me anyway. "Can the magic be tracked? Like, the individual who used it, or the spells, or something?"

Seth looked at Mariah, and they did that werewolf mind-meld thing, then Seth said, "It stops here, where Serena disappeared."

"You're sure she disappeared here?" I said.

Mariah said, "Security footage."

Which is where I came in. "I need to see it."

She opened her mouth, probably to argue, and Seth cut her off. "Show her."

A tight nod, then Mariah pivoted on a heel and stalked toward the restaurant. I followed at a slower pace. Let her work off some mad. In my experience, wolves needed all the walking off they could get.

* * *

The manager was kind enough to let us view the footage again. It didn't hurt that Seth was a well-known contributor to local charities and owned a few local businesses of various sizes.

Also, he owned the building, so there's that.

I sat at the manager's desk in a tiny nook behind the kitchen and viewed the digital footage on the manager's desktop monitor. The camera clearly showed Serena's Nissan Frontier rounding the curve in the drive-thru, between the order box and the takeout window. One car was in front of her, an older model Camry of light but otherwise indeterminate color.

Black and white video. Seriously, how much larger could color digital files be?

Another car rounded the curve, a shiny, new Jeep Wrangler, and between one breath and the next, Serena's Frontier vanished.

I blinked and clicked back, let the video play again, and yes, that's exactly what had happened. The other vehicles were in exactly the positions they should be in, as was the surrounding scenery. I played the security footage a few times, just to check, then shifted to footage from two other outdoor cameras. Serena drove up, waited in line like a patient wolf, ordered at the box. Just before that, her head was down. Texting dad while she waited for the Camry's driver to order, was my bet. Then around the curve toward the window, and poof! She was gone.

Like magic.

Uneasiness settled into me, and I rubbed my prickling nape, pondering what I'd seen. I wasn't so well-versed on magic that I knew which spell could make an entire vehicle disappear *on camera*, but I knew it would take a powerful practitioner. I'd forgotten earlier, when it occurred to me that a chaos witch might be behind this. I knew two such witches, one of whom was my brother and, like me, nearly completely blind to magic.

The other chaos witch? My mother, and from what I'd been told, she had more than enough oomph to pull off a spell of that magnitude.

FIVE

Nick texted to let me know that he'd found someone to cover my shift at Kinley's that evening, allowing me to devote that much more time to tracking down Serena. Seth and I said goodbye to Mariah in the parking lot, and he drove me to the Jimenez's house in his Tundra.

Yes, he'd won the driving war. Or rather, I'd given in because *him powerful werewolf, me puny half witch*. Kinda like Tarzan and Jane, except without the romance.

The Jimenez's house stood in a working-class neighborhood comprised of small, well-kempt lots and tidy shotgun homes built to house mill workers, back in the day when Crossville was a mill town. A willowy teen was maneuvering a push mower across the front lawn when Seth parked the Tundra at the curb. Her shoulders were stiff, her eyes dry, but her expression was caught between grief and tight anger.

Seth's nostrils flared as we exited the truck. As soon as he opened his door, the teen cut the mower's engine and parked it. She turned toward us, her spine straight as an iron rod, and faced down her father's alpha with the nerve of someone very secure in her place in life.

Her voice drifted to us, soft and high pitched. "Dad's waiting for you inside."

Seth walked to her and placed a hand on her shoulder, and her expression wavered and nearly broke.

"We'll find her," he said, and she sniffed and nodded and reeled it back in.

Envy shot through me. That's what the pack bond was like. When a wolf's strength faltered, she could draw from the strength of her pack, of her alpha. And when your alpha was as strong as Seth?

Yeah. Hard not to envy that, especially when you only had one person you could one hundred percent rely on the way Nick and I did.

But I had him, so I buried the envy and followed Seth into the Jimenez's home.

Horatio was standing in the living room when we walked in, staring blankly at the wall of framed photos hung on the wall to the left of the door. He was as spare as his younger daughter and not much taller than me, and his skin was weathered and worn from a lifetime of working construction.

"She hated mowing the yard," he said.

It took me a minute to figure out that he was talking about Serena and not her younger sibling.

"But it was her turn, you know? And now Sarah's out there because she can't stand being in here without her Sissy."

Seth held out a hand, and Horatio grabbed it and let Seth draw him close, nearly chest to chest with their hands clasped together between them. "We'll find her."

The words had the same effect on Horatio as they'd had on Sarah, calming the older man. His shoulders sagged and he exhaled a shuddering sigh and nodded, then stepped away, dropping Seth's hand.

I held out my own and shook his calloused hand. "Vanessa Kinley. Seth asked me to look into Serena's disappearance."

"He told me he would." Horatio glanced at the framed

pictures, then focused on me. His eyes were almost as black as his hair and hooded under the thin folds of his eyelids. "What do you need me to do?"

His voice held the desperate fear of a father standing too close to the edge of hopelessness. You learned to read the signs, after a while. After you'd seen enough children go missing, enough parents standing helplessly in front of a wall of pictures, wondering if they'd ever see their child again.

"May I see your text messages to and from Serena?" I said.

His gaze darted to Seth and back again. "Yeah, sure. If that will help."

He picked up his cellphone where it rested on a low coffee table sitting between a comfortable looking couch and a flat screen TV, logged in, and handed it to me.

I took it and scrolled through the text thread between them, skimming back to see what kind of relationship they had. Most of the texts were everyday fare. Serena checking in. Horatio asking her to pick up Sarah on her way home. What do you want for dinner, where's the good frying pan, I'm with friends, be home late. That sort of thing. Nothing out of the ordinary.

I took a closer look at the past twenty-four hours, ending with the messages Serena sent while she was in the drive-thru. And again, ordinary stuff. I noted the time of her last message ("Do we need ketchup?") and handed it back to him.

"Anything?" he said with enough hope in his voice that I felt like a heel for not finding the clue to where Serena was in a string of inconsequential texts.

"It's a process, sir." Which was so true as to be cliché. "May I see Serena's bedroom?"

"Down the hall. First door on the left."

I left him to talk with Seth, letting their low, masculine murmurs fade behind me as I turned into the hallway and found Serena's room. The door was cracked half a foot. I pulled my jacket sleeve down to cover the heel of my palm and used it to push the door all the way open.

The room was small, maybe ten by twelve. One window

bisected the far wall, overlooking the front yard through sheer pink curtains and blinds partially closed. A neatly made twin bed was pushed against the far wall so that the foot of the bed blocked the window. A gray and pink striped duvet and matching pillows covered the bed. No nightstand, but a bookcase filled with textbooks, framed photographs, and the ephemera of a young girl's life was placed next to the bed on the far left wall. A closet door on the right, door slightly ajar. A pressboard desk with cheap wood veneer sat in the corner beside the closet, its top covered with papers, books, pens, paperclips. A newer, nicer office chair with rollers sat a few feet away from the desk, as if Serena had pushed it back and left in a hurry.

The walls were eggshell white, their surfaces covered in unframed posters of soccer stars, school photos, ribbons, and a whiteboard with a schedule scrawled across its surface. Glow-in-the-dark stars were affixed to the ceiling above her bed, and a small telescope sat in the tiny space between the end of the bed and the wall, beyond the closet door.

Nothing was out of place. If Serena had dirty laundry, it wasn't on the floor or the bed, and other than the desk, everything was neatly arranged and organized, including the bookshelf.

It looked like what it was, the room of a young woman transitioning into adulthood who hadn't quite let her teenage years go.

The floor creaked to my left. I stepped back and turned to face Seth.

"Anything?" he said.

I shook my head. "I didn't expect to find anything here, not given the way she disappeared."

"Then why—"

"Old habits," I said firmly. "Is the rest of the house this neat?"

He glanced into Serena's bedroom, his forehead furrowed. "What's wrong with neat?"

That was the question, wasn't it? The room fit what I knew

of her from Seth. The only outliers were the stars and the telescope, but most runaways didn't leave because they were closet stargazers.

I was nearly one hundred precent sure Serena wasn't a runaway. Disappearing on camera could only be faked by stage magicians or really good video editors. I was pretty sure we could rule both out right now, unless the manager or one of the crew at the restaurant was a videographer on the side.

I made a mental note to check on that, just to cover all the bases.

The big lead here was the magic. I had a vague idea where to start with it, but only a vague one. It's not every day that I had to approach Auntie O with questions about witchcraft.

Unless it wasn't a witch at work here, which might explain the confusing nature of the magic itself.

Maybe I was grasping at straws there because I didn't want a witch to be behind Serena's disappearance. Hopefully, Auntie would have some answers for me, and if not her, maybe someone else in the supernatural community would. I still had contacts from my days with the PD. Surely I could shake some trees, get some answers.

Speaking of shaking trees.

"Mariah can't follow any of the magic she smelled?" I said.

"No." Seth's furrowed brow disappeared behind the stony mask of an alpha. "But she knows the smell now. If she ever scents it again, she'll match it."

I nodded as I reached over and pulled the door shut with my covered hand. I had one more trick up my sleeve, but I'd have to wait until the restaurant closed before I could play it.

Horatio gave me Serena's schedules for classes and work, and let me take pictures of her photographs with my phone. I asked him to go over the last twenty-four hours with me again, then Seth and I left the small family to their worry.

Seth had to go by his house for a pack thing, and I tagged

along because I didn't have a choice. That's what happened when you let a dominant drive. They never consulted you for the destination.

I let the wry thought slip away as I set aside my cellphone and the notes I'd been making and enjoyed the view. Seth's house was in a gated subdivision surrounding a high-end golf course. The houses were widely spaced and set on lots of at least three acres, most of it wooded, and one end of the course backed up to national forest. It was the perfect place for the alpha of an active, tightly knit pack to live.

Seth's house sat back from the road a good hundred feet. The concrete driveway curved slightly to the left so that part of it disappeared behind the landscaping before terminating in a rough circle in front of the house. Part of it continued around back toward the detached four-car garage and what I jokingly referred to as the activity center: A fenced-in, half-basketball court, a pool, and the entrance to the jogging trail winding throughout Seth's three point one five acre lot.

The house itself rose three stories above the driveway, a rock and wood monstrosity filled with warm, soothing colors and light. There was a basement below, I knew, but I'd never been down there. Apparently, it was reserved for pack things. Newly turned werewolves, a rec room, and the like. The whole thing was, like Kinley's, a safe space where the wolves could be themselves.

And at night, when the moon was full and the human neighbors were safely tucked in bed, the pack shed their humanity and used the golf course and surrounding woods as their playground.

Mariah was sitting outside on the shallow rockwork steps leading to the massive double front door when Seth parked the Tundra.

Just the wolf I wanted to talk to.

She stood as Seth and I got out and shut the truck's doors, and stonily ignored me. "Soup's on."

"Trudy?" he said.

Her terse nod elicited a sigh from him. No idea why, exactly. Trudy was Seth's sister. They had a close relationship, though she was human and cautious of the wolves. I didn't know her well. Nick was Seth's friend, not me. This was only the third or fourth time I'd been to his house, outside of the occasional holiday party.

"I'll talk to her." He jogged up the steps at a clip I couldn't match. I stopped at the top beside his enforcer as he reached the entrance doors, and when I didn't follow, he turned and said, "Coming?"

"Just a sec." I jerked my chin at Mariah. "Follow up question."

He grunted and entered the house, and Mariah turned an icy stare on me.

"What?" she said, her tone much less friendly than it had been a moment earlier.

Right to the point then. "Did Serena Jimenez have any conflicts within the pack?"

"We don't have conflicts."

"Why not?"

She shrugged one shoulder. "Seth doesn't allow it."

"There are tensions, though. Wolves that don't quite get along, fights for dominance, that sort of thing?"

"You writing a report?"

"I'm trying to find a missing she-wolf." My voice was as patient as hers was snappy. She was testing me, and I was not going to let her unnerve me. "You said there were no people smells in the area where Serena disappeared, only magic. What about werewolves?"

Her gaze sharpened on me in a way that made me feel like a rabbit in an open field: prey. "You're saying one of our pack did this?"

"I'm asking," I said, still calm as a cloudless sky, "if you smelled any werewolves, since people smells and werewolf smells are likely very different."

The question took her unawares, and she reined in the

unspoken threat. "They are. People are...fussy. Unnatural. Too many smells at once."

"And werewolves?"

"Wild, like the forest. Musky." Her nose twitched once, her nostrils flared, and her shoulders relaxed. "Like digging in loam versus standing on asphalt."

That made way more sense than it should've, all things considered. "Were any wolves around the restaurant when Serena disappeared?"

"No fresh scents." She rolled her shoulders, twitched her nose. "Old ones. Familiar ones."

"Wolves you know?"

"Pack wolves, yeah. But they wouldn't—"

"Kidnap one of their own in a way that made a vehicle disappear off security footage?"

The ghost of a grim smile flitted around her mouth and was gone just as quickly. "There would've been blood."

I could only hope I never saw that. "Thank you."

She grunted and turned away from me, giving me her back while she scanned the surrounding property.

Which told me exactly how much of a threat she considered me.

I shook my head ruefully and walked inside. Puny half witch with only one spell under her belt, and that a closely guarded secret. No wonder Mariah dismissed me so easily. I would've laughed if she weren't within hearing range.

SIX

The foyer was empty when I walked in. It was a small space, for the size of the house, with gleaming hardwood floors and original landscapes hung on the subtly colored walls. I followed the sounds of men talking toward the right through a comfortably furnished TV room, bypassing the staircase leading to the upper floors.

My bootheels were uncomfortably loud against the floors, even on the large carpets strategically placed to protect the polished wood from furniture and the pitter patter of humans and wolves. I'd always liked Seth's house. The rooms were cozy and inviting, for all their size. The TV room alone could easily hold ten to fifteen people on the large sofas and chairs without anyone feeling crowded.

That was a small group, though. I had no idea how large the pack was, exactly, but I knew more than fifteen wolves were members. Add in their families and you were looking at two or three times that number.

I found Seth in the kitchen, sitting at the central island with Miles, his financial lieutenant, and Jamal, his training lieutenant, bracketing him. Trudy stood at the stove with her back to the doorway, stirring the steaming contents of a large pot with a wooden spoon.

I loved this kitchen. Lots of space, lots of light, a huge pantry tucked away in an unobvious place, and it always smelled like freshly baked bread.

My favorite part of Seth's house lay beyond this room. A door to the left of the main cooking area opened onto a patio with a bonfire pit, a large grill, and plenty of outdoor seating, both on the patio itself and around the pool. Unlike the larger swimming pool that was part of the community's rec area, this pool was rocked in and filled with fresh, unchlorinated water kept clean through some trick of human ingenuity. Ferns and other native plants had been planted strategically around it, lending it a natural feel. It was placed near the edge of the woods on the back side of the property and, at least to my eye, served as a transitional point between the house and the forest.

I stepped into the kitchen and sat at a six-seater farmhouse style table placed to the left of the entrance. No one bothered turning around, likely because they all knew who it was. The werewolves had probably smelled or heard me coming, and Seth would've told Trudy to expect me.

"We searched the roadsides," Jamal said. "Every possible route. Nothing."

Seth nodded once. "Expand the search. Cut off a team to cover the river."

I stifled a tired sigh. The West Mill River ran along the edge of town and eventually dumped into the Chattahoochee farther to the southeast, below Lake Lanier. Compared to the 'Hooch, it wasn't much of a river, though its placid, murky waters were still wide and deep enough to canoe and kayak. Once or twice a year, someone drowned in it, or came close, but it was safe enough, if you respected the water.

"Yes, boss," Jamal said as he rose and turned to leave. He was a big man, easily topping Seth by half a foot or more, with the calm, icy gaze of an old, old wolf. His skin was so black, it glinted purple in the right light, and a faint, lilting accent underscored his words.

I'd never gotten a good feel for him. He wasn't aloof, but he wasn't friendly either, and he treated everyone equally, except Seth and me. Seth, he was respectful to. Me, he ignored.

Right then, his gaze touched mine as he walked past, something he'd never done before. Usually, he ignored me to the point of not acknowledging my presence in any way unless circumstance forced him to.

I tried not to let that bother me. Of all Seth's wolves, Mariah and Jamal were the only two I didn't get along with. It's not that I didn't get along with Jamal. He exuded the kind of quiet surety I was attracted to, and he was handsome, too, with even features and a strong build. Throw in the dangerous predator air lurking behind his dark gaze and he had a definite *wow* factor I found hard to ignore.

There was a spark there, I admit, but if it was reciprocated, he hadn't once let on. Too bad. My dating prospects were sparse to nil and showed no signs of improving in the near future. The one and only guy I'd gone out with this year had left a bad taste in my mouth. I wasn't ready to date again, and I sure as tooting wasn't going to flirt with a disinterested werewolf. Any woman that desperate for a date was just begging to be rejected, or worse.

I waited until Jamal's quiet footsteps receded before turning my attention back to the conversation. Miles was updating Seth on recent rogue activity, something I would've expected Mariah, as Seth's enforcer, to have a better grasp of.

But what did I know? I wasn't a member of the pack, merely an occasional observer.

Trudy pulled loaves of bread out of the oven, turned them out on a waiting dishtowel, and thumped their bottoms, testing for doneness. A moment later, she retrieved a stack of ceramic bowls from a glass-fronted cabinet and ladled soup into two. When she turned to set the bowls on the island in front of the men, her gaze caught mine and held.

Now, normally Trudy and I get along just fine. She's not the most outgoing person. Then again, neither am I. But we were friendly enough that we smiled and chitchatted whenever we were thrown together.

Today, the expression she turned on me was so much like one of Seth's, it threw me. They looked alike, sure, though Trudy was a handful of years older and willowy to Seth's rock wall build. But I'd never seen her look like at anyone like that, as if they were a suspect in a double homicide.

My cop instincts kicked in and I leveled a steady, hardnosed gaze at her. I'd done nothing wrong and was there to help. Most certainly, I didn't deserve to be treated with such wary suspicion.

She flipped her long, chestnut colored braid over her shoulder and dropped her gaze as she returned to her task, leaving me to wonder exactly what had gone through her mind when she saw me.

I turned down Seth's offer of soup, not because of Trudy's odd behavior, but because we'd just eaten a few hours before. He might have the metabolism of a werewolf. I did not.

Miles was kind enough to bring his soup to the table and sit with me. He and I chatted about Serena's disappearance for a while, then about the neighborhood and Crossville's upcoming annual fall festival. I told him Nick was planning something at Kinley's, which he did every year. The bar faced Main Street. Participation was very nearly a requirement.

Miles even offered me some of his bread, which I took because, damn it, these people were my friends, as much as they could be friends with non-werewolves. I liked Miles and the other wolves, even Mariah. Ok, I had a healthy respect for Mariah, but still. Nick and I had always been on friendly terms with the pack.

Trudy's expression must've bothered me more than I'd initially thought.

The sun hung low above the distant mountains by the time Seth finished eating. I said my goodbyes to Trudy, Miles, and the other pack members that had drifted in, then had Seth take me back to my office. He parked on the street under a glowing lamplight and left the Tundra idling.

Abruptly, he said, "I should come with you."

I glanced at him, surprised. "You need to be with the pack. I can handle my end."

His hands gripped the steering wheel. Lean hands, surprisingly dexterous fingers. Not the hands of a man who'd taken his father's construction business and turned it into a small empire. "I don't think you should be alone."

I bit back a laugh, more touched by his concern than I wanted to admit, and patted his bare forearm. "I've got it, Seth. I promise."

His left hand dropped to mine, holding it against his skin, though his gaze stayed front and center. For a moment, I thought he was going to say something, then he shook his head and let me go.

"Be careful," he said.

"You, too. I'll let you know if I find anything."

He grunted, and I slid out of the truck and waited on the sidewalk while he drove away.

I should've gone right in, maybe would've if everyone weren't suddenly acting so strange. First Trudy, then Jamal, and now Seth. Who was next?

I really shouldn't've thought that, because doing so conjured up the man walking across the street toward me in the full shadows of night. He was average in every way. Average height, average build, average and completely forgettable features, which turned out to be an advantage when you made your living hunting lowlifes.

My heart sank to my stomach as the man stepped onto the sidewalk and stopped six feet away.

"Hey, Kinley," he said. "I hear you've got a missing she-wolf on your hands. Mind if we talk inside?"

Resigned, I dug my keys out, unlocked my office door, and led my old partner from the Crossville PD into my office.

SEVEN

I flipped on the lights and let the door go, hoping he'd take the hint and go home. Or at least leave me alone with the music already thumping inside Kinley's.

"What do you want, Peterson?" I said as I stalked through the reception area toward my desk.

"What I always want. To solve a case." The door closed and the lock clicked into place, then his footsteps followed mine toward the back. "What do you have so far?"

"Nothing yet, but I anticipate a headache will pop up the minute you ask another question."

"Always a smartass," he said, his voice mild.

I plopped down behind my desk, facing him. He looked older somehow than the last time I'd seen him, the day I handed in my badge and gun and resigned from the force. An extra line or two radiated from the corners of his eyes, a touch more gray colored his dishwater blonde hair. Maybe there were an extra couple of pounds around his midsection, but I doubt anyone else would notice. We'd been partners for two years, me and Peterson, working together so often his wife accused me of being the other woman.

I hadn't been. Ever. Rick Peterson was a lot of things. A

hard-souled cop with a nose for sniffing out the truth. A misogynist of the first order when it came to women on the force, or with me anyway. But a cheater? Never.

"Serena Jimenez," he prompted.

I arched an eyebrow. "What about her?"

"Our missing she-wolf."

He made a show of pulling a pen and a battered notebook out of the inside pocket of his canvas jacket. It was clean, too, and as neat as the rest of him. That's the other thing about Rick. He wasn't a slob, which begged the question as to why his wife had left him. Half the guys on the force couldn't find their dicks without their wives showing them where it was. Rick was not among them.

Not that I'd had personal experience with finding his dick.

I pushed the toe of my boot into the plastic guard covering the carpet under my chair, swiveling it and me around. "I'm confused. What's a she-wolf? Been watching a lot of documentaries on NatGeo lately?"

"A she-wolf. Otherwise known as a female werewolf." He said it slowly and with a touch of humor, like he knew exactly which game I was playing and why. "One of Seth Rhone's pack."

I pulled my boot up, stopping the chair in mid-swivel. "I know Seth. Good friend of my brother Nick. You remember Nick, don't you, Peterson?"

"I remember having a talk with him about assaulting a police officer after his fist made its acquaintance with my nose. That'd be about a year ago now, right? The day after you turned in your badge?"

I stared at him, refusing to rise to the bait. Let him try to toy with me. My younger, more naïve self, fresh out of the academy, might've answered him with quivering self-righteousness. The older, more cynical me had five years of service under her belt and knew better.

Peterson stood and fished a peppermint out of the Frankenstein mug sitting on a corner of my desk. "Not gonna talk about the local pack, huh? Guess I'll have to interview

Rhone instead."

"What're you interviewing Seth about again?"

"Missing coeds. Werewolves."

"Oh, right. Malformed creatures howling at the moon and all that jazz." I whirled a finger in a circle around my temple. "Maybe you should have your doctor up your meds."

"Maybe so." He turned and said, without looking back, "You were a better liar when you were a cop, Kinley."

I shot a bird at his back and let him walk out without saying another word to him.

It took the better part of twenty minutes for me to calm down. Good thing, as I figured my old partner was waiting outside for me to leave so he could follow me and try to scoop my case.

Not that I needed him. I'd never needed him to solve a case. He was the only person in the world who'd never acknowledged my skills as a detective, the only one who'd doubted my abilities. It still rankled. Partners were supposed to have each other's backs, like family. And he hadn't had mine.

I'd never hidden anything from him, ever. When the Captain sent me out on a supernatural call, Peterson went with me. He knew werewolves existed, even if we'd never talked about it. Maybe he knew I was a witch, too. We'd never talked about that either.

I sucked in a breath and blew it out, hard. *Bitter much, Kinley?* I asked myself, and cut it off right there. Maybe I wasn't a cop anymore. Maybe leaving the force hadn't been entirely my decision. But I was still a good investigator and Serena Jimenez was still missing.

When enough time had passed for Peterson to get bored...

No, bored wasn't the right word. He'd never gotten bored on a stakeout. The man was as patient as a saint.

But enough time had passed for him to think I'd settled into work.

I checked my witchy kit for the work I needed to do. A

piece of chalk, a compass made of an old nail and cotton thread, a squirt bottle full of purified water, and a small, tattered piece of paper with a stylized rune painted on it in black watercolor.

Back in my detective days, I'd stored those items in a zippered pencil holder in my car, ready to use whenever I needed them. These days, most of my cases were mundane. Insurance fraud required legwork, not magic.

A missing person? Now, that fit well with my one magic trick.

I snuck out the back door. Ok, I didn't sneak, I walked, but whatever. Very few knew that the backdoor for my office opened into a hallway that, in turn, connected every other room in the building in one way or another.

Originally, this building had been a warehouse-style factory, built back in the days when cotton mills popped up in every third town across the South. Seth bought it decades after the textile industry shifted overseas, taking its jobs with it. He'd converted it into a two-floored, mixed use building right around the time that Crossville's Tourism and Industry Board had been trying to revitalize the town. Instead of backing each newly created room on the first floor against each other, he'd inserted a hallway down the middle for use as a service entrance.

He'd even been kind enough to place two stairwells inside for the renters in the upstairs apartments, of which Nick and I were only two of several. Nick used ours all the time to go between his apartment and Kinley's. I preferred pretending like I didn't live and work in the same building.

The downstairs service hallway was dead useful, though. I slipped into it now, locked the office's back door behind me, and turned left. The door at the end of the hall led to the interior stairwell and Kinley's back office, and beyond that, the kitchen and the bar proper.

I went through and noted that yes, indeed, it might be barely seven on a Saturday, but the place was already packed. Game on, I figured. Football something.

I let Nick know where I was going and why on my way out,

then stepped onto the sidewalk running down this side of Main Street and scanned the street for Peterson. Didn't see his car, an older model Buick sedan that was as nondescript as he was. Probably, and this was pure assumption, but probably, he'd parked on Winfield and waited for me there. Which left me free and clear to jog across Main and retrieve my car, a Honda Accord, from the parking deck across the street.

Also, conveniently enough, owned by Mr. Seth Rhone, alpha werewolf and all-around good buddy.

Fifteen minutes later, I parked at the restaurant where Serena had disappeared. My timing was off, which I would've known if Peterson hadn't distracted me. I went through the drive-thru and ordered a burger all the way, fries, a drink, and plenty of napkins, please, then parked across the street at a bank where I had a good view of the restaurant. By the time I finished eating, the air held a distinct nip and the restaurant had closed for the night. Half an hour after that, the last employee out locked the doors and drove away.

I moved my car to the restaurant's parking lot, gathered up my trash and threw it away, and took my witchy tools to the spot where Serena's truck had vanished. The security cameras were still on (I'd checked earlier), but that was fine. If anyone cared to look, all they'd see was me drawing stuff on the pavement.

I pulled out the compass and chalk first and used those to inscribe a rough circle around the approximate space I was targeting. The circle didn't really do anything other than help me focus what little magic I possessed.

Next came the piece of paper with the rune painted on it. Using it as a guide, I drew the rune straight onto the asphalt, concentrating hard on what I wanted to see. I'd found the rune in some of the things Auntie O saved for us after Mom disappeared, when I'd been a rebellious snot and wanted to do some damage.

By then, Nick and I knew that Mom was a witch, and I understood exactly what runes were used for as Auntie had explained them to us during the brief time when she'd tested our magical mettle. The rune had once been part of a grimoire. I'd ripped it off because I liked it. It had very nearly ended up as a tattoo on one of my private parts.

What? I already confessed my rebellious snot inclinations.

Anyway, I tested it first on Nick because I wasn't sure what magic the rune called. Grimoires weren't always clear on that, since they were compiled by witches who, generally speaking, already knew what the spells were for. There hadn't even been a title.

I'd gotten lucky in unknowingly choosing a mostly benign rune, this one being a key for illumination. If the magic had run more strongly in my blood, I might have gotten a ball of light or something. Instead, my puny magic had called forth a ghostly, faintly pink image of Nick staring at his phone.

The image had lasted maybe a second before it faded, but I was hooked. Over the years, I refined my techniques through experimentation and hit on the focusing circle, which allowed the ghostly illumination to linger long enough to be helpful. My little rune spell had come in handy in my cop days, and I never regretted cribbing it and learning how to use it.

But sometimes I think back to my first try and thank Heaven that I didn't inadvertently blow Nick up or turn him into a frog or something.

When I finished etching the rune into the pavement, I put my tools away and placed one palm flat against the rune, covering it completely. I closed my eyes and concentrated on Serena. Would've been easier if I'd met her, but having Seth, Horatio, and Sarah's voices fresh in my head ran a close second. I pulled their descriptions to the front of my mind, letting them overlap each other and the pictures I'd memorized. A formal head shot taken during Serena's senior year of high school. Another of her smiling after a soccer game with her arms slung around her teammates. A couple more I'd seen at the Jimenez's.

The pavement warmed beneath my palm, and my skin started to tingle.

"Show me," I whispered, then my eyes flew open and I *saw*.

Pink light curled from under my palm, spiraling outward until it filled the circle, then climbing up as if the circle contained it. The truck's hood appeared first, a shimmering outline with pink magic glimmering across it in thin, irregular waves like lightning bugs flashing in tandem. Then the steering wheel. Hands tightly gripping it. Serena glancing to her left, her hair swinging around with the gesture. The passenger door opening and a hand reaching inside.

Then something appeared between Serena and the intruding hand, something belonging to neither her nor whomever was getting in her truck.

My mother's face.

The image startled me so much, I lifted my hand off the rune, breaking the spell. The image shimmered and disappeared before I could tell who the intruder was. I would've cursed my lack of focus, except my mind held only one thought:

What the hell, Mom.

EIGHT

More out of habit than anything, I squirted water over the chalk rune, washing it away so no unsuspecting human would stumble across it and accidentally trigger the magic. Some humans did possess latent magic. Once Nick and I knew that magic was a thing, Auntie O drilled it into us that we must never, ever leave spells laying around.

Something Mom should've told us a long, long time ago.

I shoved the automatic bitterness down as I gathered up my tools and trudged back to my car. As soon as I opened the door and stored my witchy tools, I whipped out my cellphone and texted Auntie with a quick, *Gotta talk asap, re: Mom.*

Almost immediately, she texted back. *Lunch tomorrow @ 1. Bring Nicky.*

I sighed. Damn. He was going to kill me for getting him up that early after a Saturday night working the bar.

Oh, well. This was important. In the illumination, Mom hadn't been the one reaching into Serena's truck through the passenger door. Her body hadn't been there, but her face...

I closed my eyes and pulled the memory of the illumination up, recalling as many details as I could. The narrow rectangle of her face, the thin nose, the elegant sweep of her dancer's neck, the fall of blonde hair around her face and shoulders. Wideset eyes staring through me.

Her expression. Stark, tense. Waiting.

A driver honked their horn nearby, startling me out of the mini meditation, and Mom's face faded from my mind. The moon had risen while I was standing there, contemplating the meaning of the illumination.

Useless speculation. The picture was incomplete, the puzzle of Serena's disappearance, and Mom's, a sketchy outline at best. I needed more information, more data. More clues besides a ghostly arm reaching through a truck around the time the vehicle disappeared.

An arm with a masculine hand.

I tucked that information away and got in my car while dialing Seth. Maybe his werewolves had found some trace of Serena during their search of Crossville and its environs.

The bar was in full swing when I got back. Music and laughter spilled out of the door, and through the windows, I could see Nick tending the bar, his capable hands working his own brand of magic.

My brief brush with magic had worn me out, so I bypassed the crowd, retrieved my laptop from my office, and headed to my apartment using the outside entrance.

If Peterson had stuck around, I didn't see him. Pity. I had a question or two for him, now that I'd had time to process our conversation.

Missing coeds, he'd said.

Had he inadvertently dropped a clue, or…?

No. Peterson never let a purposeless word slip out of his mouth. He'd wanted me to know Serena wasn't the only missing kid, though what he'd hoped to gain from me other than rattling my cage, I didn't know. He was the cop. The Crossville PD didn't have the resources of police departments in larger districts, but they still had access to things I didn't.

I did have the internet, however, and I knew how to use it.

Once home, I changed into sweats and an old t-shirt, turned on the latest episode of *The Blacklist* from the DVR, and settled onto the couch with my feet propped up and my laptop open. My first instinct was to hit the local newspaper, which wouldn't do me any good since I read the weekly rag and Nick kept up with it on Facebook. I would remember him telling me if people had been reported missing.

Unless it hadn't been reported.

On impulse, I logged into a supernatural forum fronted by a preppers' website. The website was real and downright handy. Supes received a ten percent discount right off the top, plus free shipping on orders over fifty dollars, not something offered to the general public. I bought my tactical clothes through there because they offered a range of sizes outside the norms found at human shops.

The forum was similar to the granularity of reddit, just tailored to supernatural interests rather than human ones. Different kinds of witches could follow the main witch topic, or the one for their specific specialty, or they could subscribe to grimoires, a spell ingredients swap, or charm making, to name a few.

Honestly, there were so many topics for witches, I could barely keep up. Throw in the general topics plus the ones specific to different species and it was overwhelming. When I'd been with the PD, I'd made an effort to keep up because it was part of my job. Once I'd struck out on my own, though, I'd pruned back the topics I followed to the ones that interested me most.

Now, I skipped over my notifications and went straight to the search function. A few clicks later and I was scrolling through posts on missing supernaturals.

No, it wasn't that easy. It's not like there was a missing supernaturals topic. You had to know what you were looking for. Supes were cagey about their personal lives. The more sensitive the topic, the cagier they got. Missing friends and family? A definite sore spot.

Leave aside that a supernatural on its own was, generally speaking, more vulnerable without the protection of its clan, even if the clan consisted of only two entities. Witch hunts, literal or otherwise, weren't uncommon in the twenty-first century; they were just hidden better.

And not. Social media and ubiquitous camera phones made it a lot harder for an unwary supernatural to fit in. Those were the ones that usually got targeted, which was why the Fair Folk hid behind their magically protected fairy mounds. I'd never seen one and had no wish to. Dangerous creatures, were the Fae, dangerous and unable to blend among the more populous human species. It was a nasty combination.

I flipped through the search results, skimming for keywords. Many of the posts referred to old disappearances. Some had been resolved. Others were too far from Crossville to be of real interest. Many didn't have a name attached. Names held power, and true names were rarely shared, especially by the older, more powerful creatures.

Then a familiar name caught my eye and my breath hitched. *Galena Kinley.* Mom!

I checked the date, did a rough mental calculation, and frowned. She'd crafted a carefully worded post around mine and Nick's first birthday looking for one Mirek Novotny. The hairs on the back of my neck prickled and I shivered. We'd never known our father. Mom said they'd had a brief affair and she'd never bothered telling him she was pregnant.

That's it, the sum total of what I knew about him. A name, an affair, a decision made.

And now this.

I hit CTRL P, sending the post to my printer for a hard copy, then returned to the search results. Half an hour and three variant searches later, I'd found two other female supernaturals that had gone missing in the past six months in the Greater Atlanta area, one a sixteen-year-old witch named Heather, the other a born vampire in her mid-twenties named Willow. The former had just started her junior year at a community college on the west side of Atlanta. Skipped ahead a few grades, apparently. The latter was working on her doctorate at Georgia Tech.

Quickly, I printed those two posts off, then set aside my laptop and stood into a stretch. Three missing females did not a trend make, especially if nothing tied them together. Being a supernatural didn't count. So many species, so many possibilities. I'd check into it regardless. At this point, every lead had to be tracked down.

The *Blacklist* episode ended, and I checked the time, yawning as I stood and stretched. Midnight. Time for a quick snack, then maybe another couple of hours searching. I padded into the kitchen, half my mind on the missing women, the other half spinning uselessly about Mom's two and a half decades old post.

The next day, I drove a suitably grumpy Nicky across town to Auntie O's, going slow because someone had had a date after getting off work and had a mild hangover to show for it. Not to mention any names, but his initials were Nick Kinley.

I snickered under my breath, earning a grunt from him.

"Shuddup," he said.

I glanced over, grinning. He was wedged into the Accord's seat with his knees pushed uncomfortably against the dash and his arms crossed over his chest. Sunglasses covered his eyes, though I knew they were closed against the perfect October sky.

"Almost there," I said, injecting just the right amount of cheer into the words to annoy him.

He shifted in his seat, trying to get comfortable. "Get a bigger car."

"We could've driven your truck."

"Forget it," he said around yawn, then added gruffly, "Drive your own car."

My snicker turned into a guffaw. Poor thing. He needed more sleep.

My laughter faded as I turned into Auntie's neighborhood and slowed. I hadn't told Nick about last night's illumination spell, though he was well aware that I used it. Auntie O didn't, and therein lay the problem. She'd warned us away from magic so many times since giving up on teaching us.

There was no way around telling her. I needed to know what Mom's face meant, needed to get some feedback on Dimitri's request and that old post Mom had written. I needed help. If confessing to using what was essentially a harmless spell got me that help, then so be it.

Auntie's house was a cheery cottage straight out of the English countryside, a place I was relatively certain she'd never been. Even now, when autumn had a good hold on the city and the trees were turning bright fall colors, her yard looked like a mystical fairy tale full of color. Every time I visited, I expected to spot a tiny Tinkerbell flitting among the flowers.

Sadly, it hadn't happened yet, but I still looked.

Auntie had left the front door open for us, with the screen door shut to discourage bees from entering. I bounced up the concrete steps, painted bright blue to match the shutters, and opened the door, hollering, "Hello there, Auntie!"

Nick grumbled under his breath as he caught the screen door and stepped inside behind me.

I ignored him in favor of inhaling the rich scents of freshly baked bread mingling with cinnamon, bayberry, and eucalyptus. Rosemary! I just refrained from rubbing my hands together gleefully as I walked through the tiny living room with its ancient rugs covering hardwood floors, surrounded by faded pictures of those who'd touched Auntie's life over her six and a half decades. She had rosemary breaded pork chops in the oven. My favorite.

I went straight to the kitchen, figuring she'd be cooking. Sure enough, she was standing at the stove with her back to us, sniffing the contents of a sauce pot. Auntie's slender figure had whittled away to skin and bone over the years and her snow-white hair fell in a tangled mess of wild curls down her back. She wore a peasant blouse in a cheery kaleidoscope of blues and greens over frayed jeans, and she'd stuffed her socked feet into Birkenstocks. A late-blooming sprig of fresh lavender was tucked into her hair above the slender hairbow pulling her hair back from her bird-like face.

I relaxed into a smile as soon as I saw her. It was good to be home.

"Hey, Auntie," I said as Nick dropped into a chair at the round table on the far end of the room, by a wall of windows overlooking the back garden. "What's brewing today?"

She turned and arched an eyebrow at me. Her eyes were a lively blue behind the round, oversized glasses she wore. The frames matched her top and had small rhinestones pasted onto the arms.

"Will you never tire of that old joke, Vanessa Ann?" she said.

I grinned and leaned a hip against the sink, just out of her reach. "What old joke? It was a serious question."

"Turnip greens." She turned back to the stove and poked a wooden spoon into the pot. "Roasted potatoes and pork chops in the oven, little miss, and a cherry pie for our local barkeep."

"You're the best, Auntie," Nick said.

"You're looking a mite peaked." She was looking at him now, and though her face was turned away from me, I imagined she had both eyebrows raised. "Are you taking those vitamins I gave you? Where's my hug?"

Nick obediently rose and shambled to her, then lifted her into a giant bear hug, spoon and all. She shrieked and slapped her free hand at him, and I grabbed the spoon and took her place at the stove. Let them play. I was happy to listen.

Lunch was as chaotic as usual. Auntie asked a million questions in some random order that made sense only to her, jumping gracefully from topic to topic and back again without missing a beat. She'd taken the time to cover the battered breakfast table with a bright pumpkin tablecloth and had pulled out the company plates, but the meal felt just like so many others we'd shared since she showed up at our door the day after Mom left and took us into her home.

I might never know why. We probably would've been fine in the human foster system, given our relative lack of witchiness. Or another supernatural could've taken us in. Maybe a distant cousin or something.

But Auntie was the one who'd shown up when we'd called the emergency number tacked to the fridge, and I would always be grateful for her.

I'd just finished eating my third pork chop when Auntie set her fork down and turned a piercing stare on me.

"What happened with the pointy teeth?" she said.

I set my own fork down and patted my mouth with a napkin before answering. "A vampire showed up the night before your warning wanting me to find Mom. She's disappeared again."

Auntie sucked in a breath, but all she said was, "I distinctly saw a different sort of pointy teeth."

Nick jumped in. "Seth Rhone came by yesterday morning. Missing werewolf."

I hummed under my breath. "He asked me to help track her down."

"A missing werewolf." Auntie's eyes dropped to her napkin. She folded it carefully and tucked it between the edge of her plate and the table. "You agreed to help."

"Yes. Of course."

"Good. You're needed there. But your mother. And that vampire."

Auntie's fingers toyed with the napkin, settling it just so, then pulling it out and tucking it away again.

I glanced at Nick. Auntie could be a tad flighty, but she wasn't one to evade.

"What about the vampire?" I said.

Her mouth compressed into a thin line, nearly disappearing into the paleness of her skin. "I need to consult the bones. Perhaps a phone call. Did Serena have any witch blood in her?"

It took me a moment to catch up to her conversational jumps. "I'll ask Seth."

"No, no. The bones."

Abruptly, Auntie stood and flitted out of the room, snagging two of my discarded pork chop bones on her way past me.

Nick watched her go, his frown as deep as mine. "What was that about?"

"I don't know, but I think we should follow her." Especially since she took bones from my plate.

"Yeah." Nick laid down his napkin, glanced mournfully at the cherry pie still sitting on the counter. "Yeah. We should check on her."

"The pie isn't going anywhere."

He grunted and stood, then he and I walked through the twisting hallways of Auntie's house toward her spell room, a nook off her bedroom where she stored her witchy items. Books on divination and the like, tools of her trade, dried plants and other ephemera needed for some of her more complex spells. That sort of thing.

She even had an honest to goodness crystal ball, though she never used it. Too finicky, she claimed. One flaw in the glass could distort the vision, ruining the practitioner's ability to interpret it correctly.

Now she stood at the tiny, square table set in the middle of the room with its corners aligned to the cardinal directions. A cast iron skillet sat on the table. As Nick and I entered the room, Auntie dropped the bones into the skillet and touched a match to them. When I drew near, I noticed the shavings of wood under the bones. Those caught flame and smoke drifted upward. A moment later, the bones had charred to a crisp as if they'd been barbecued instead of touched by a small flame.

Magic. Gotta love it.

Auntie waved a hand over the flames, and they disappeared, then she pulled one of the bones out and examined it. I crossed my arms under my breasts and bit my tongue. She'd never forbidden us from watching her work, but we'd learned early on not to interrupt her. Still, the longer she looked, the tenser I got, and the tenser I got, the bigger the bad feeling in my stomach grew.

Finally, she dropped the bones and glanced up at me. "Should've used the scapula."

"The what?" Nick said.

"You know very well what a scapula is, Nicolaus. Unfortunately, I didn't buy the entire pig when I picked up the pork chops from the butcher."

I hadn't wanted to eat an entire pig, either. Not that I was going to say so when she was in divination mode. "What did you see?"

"Trouble." She picked up the skillet and handed it to Nick. "Be a dear and dispose of the bones."

Nick sighed and walked out, skillet in hand.

"And get yourself some pie while you're in the kitchen," Auntie called after him. We listened to his footsteps recede down the hallway, then Auntie turned to me. "The vampire isn't to be trusted."

"Tell me something I don't know," I said.

"He's not a run of the mill vampire searching for his next meal." Her voice held an unusual touch of fear. "Not to be trusted. Do you understand?"

I nodded, and she rushed on.

"Avoid him whenever you can. Your mother, too. And those werewolves."

"Auntie," I said gently. "I can't avoid the werewolves. Seth is our landlord. I promised I'd help him find Serena."

Her hands fluttered around her chest, then settled onto the table, her fingers tapping nervously against the wooden surface. "It doesn't make sense. The bones. The vision."

"What vision?"

"A hand reaching toward something I couldn't see."

I opened my mouth to tell her about the illumination when she said, "A pink hand, shimmery as if light reflected on it. What kind of hand is that shade of pink?"

I closed my mouth and swallowed. Well, damn. I guess I was going to have to tell her about the illumination spell after all.

NINE

bout that," I said. "So there's this rune."

Her gaze flew to mine. "Oh, no. Tell me you didn't."

I inhaled a deep breath. In for a penny. "Since I was sixteen."

Her expression tightened into true fear. "You were never supposed to dabble with the magic, Vanessa. *Never.* I warned you not to touch it."

"It's just a little spell, Auntie."

"There's no such thing as a little spell." The words boomed out of her like an unexpected roll of thunder on a cloudless day. "You must not *dabble.* I've told you a million times. Your mother told you."

"What does Mom have to do with this?"

"You have no understanding of the consequences, darling. None! We tried to protect you, and now this. The bones don't lie."

"I don't even know what the bones said!"

She raised a single finger. "Trouble. I told you."

"What *kind* of trouble?" My breath rushed out of me in a frustrated sigh. "All the spell does is show me a small moment in time. That's it."

She gasped and, if it was possible, paled. "You used an unknown illumination rune? Vanessa Ann. How could you? The consequences! This could ruin everything!"

"I don't even know what I've done." I snapped. "You haven't told me anything concrete."

"Nessie," Nick said, just loud enough to interrupt my mad. He was standing in the doorway holding a dessert plate with a half-eaten piece of cherry pie on it in one hand and a fork in the other. "What's going on?"

"She used magic!" Auntie said, at the same time that I said, "She's gone crazy!"

"I knew she was using magic," he said to Auntie, then he looked at me and mouthed, *Behave.*

I swear, a part of me wanted to cross my arms over my chest and say, "She started it." But I knew Nick was right. Auntie wasn't just our surrogate mother. She was my friend, and she deserved some respect whether she made sense or not.

"You knew." Auntie placed a hand over her heart, staggered to the room's lone chair, and sank into it. "How could you keep this from me? After all the things we've been through. After all the *warnings*! How could you use magic? And you *knew*."

It took a talented woman to lambast both of us in a single breath.

I took a deep breath of my own and let the rest of my anger go. Frustration, really. Auntie could never hit the point with a straight line. No, she had to circle around it until she'd hit every point along the way and then some. Sometimes I wished she could be straightforward, but if she ever were, I'd immediately rush her to the healer to see what was wrong.

Nick stepped into the room and handed off his pie. "I've got this," he said quietly.

It was all I could do not to throw up my hands in exasperation. Especially since Auntie had taken to rocking back and forth on the chair with her eyes tightly closed while she muttered, "Trouble now. What to do? How could she? And he *knew*!"

When she got like that, Nick was the only one who could calm her down. I took his pie and exited stage left, straight to the kitchen and my own piece of pie, though I suspected the knot in my stomach would keep me from eating another bite.

Nick came out an hour later, well after I'd finished putting lunch away and tidying the kitchen. He sat down at the table across from me and said, "She's resting."

I scowled at him. "I should be the one resting."

"Want me to slip an anxiety charm under your pillow, too?"

"No," I grumbled. "Maybe."

He chuckled softly, and I resumed staring out the window at Auntie's backyard. She'd planted a potager around the back steps and suspended intricately carved and painted bird feeders from hooks in various places among the herbs and vegetables. Beyond, a gnarled apple tree spread its branches over a far corner. Birds and butterflies flitted among the dying leaves, and bees swarmed around the square, white hives placed underneath by a local apiarist. It was late for bees. Late for butterflies, too. That never stopped Auntie from planting for them.

"What's wrong?" Nick said into the silence that had fallen between us.

"This case. The missing werewolf." I sighed and turned to him, putting the fairy tale garden out of my mind. "Missing supernaturals. I found two more."

"My God," he breathed. "Why hadn't we heard about them?"

I shook my head, pressed stiff fingers to the headache gathering behind my eyes. "They didn't live near Crossville. I was hoping Auntie could shed some light on the case. On the illumination I witnessed."

"She had to've seen something useful."

"Oh, I'm sure she did. What, though? That's the key."

One corner of his mouth turned up into a rueful smile. "Let me guess. She flitted from topic to topic."

"As usual." I let my hand drop, though the pain hadn't ebbed. For some unknown reason, the cut on my wrist chose that moment to throb in time to the pain in my head. I pressed a thumb over it, hoping it would just go away as I continued. "She's worried about something."

"Obvs, Nessie. You shouldn't have told her you were using magic."

"You say that like I'm doing meth," I snapped, then reeled it in on a long inhale. "Sorry."

He grunted, which I took as a combination *don't worry about it* and *what else?*

"She kept mentioning the vampire," I said. "And the wolves, warning me to stay away from them. Trouble, she said, but she could never pin down exactly what kind of trouble."

"Again, obvs." He spread his hands in a half shrug. "They're deadly, dangerous supernatural creatures, the exact sort of trouble she's been warning us away from since we were kids."

"Except she was the one who introduced us to the supernatural community." I glanced again at the late afternoon sun warming Auntie's back yard, then stood. "If she's asleep, we should go. I need to check in with Seth and try to figure out what Mom was doing in my illumination."

Nick's eyes went round as saucers and he nearly choked on his next breath. "You didn't say anything about seeing Mom in the magic."

"Auntie didn't give me a chance."

Which is what I got for coming to her instead of one of my other sources. The difference was, I trusted Auntie. Whatever she thought of my use of magic, once she calmed down, she'd help me sort through it. I had a feeling Serena and the other missing young women didn't have that kind of time left, but other supernaturals weren't always so trustworthy.

Still. I had to do something.

Nick left a note for Auntie on scrap paper rummaged from a drawer, then we headed back downtown, my investigation no farther along than when we'd arrived.

TEN

I spent the rest of the afternoon and evening chasing down leads. No classes on Sunday, so that was out, which left Seth and the other missing young women. Seth's wolves had found nothing. No vehicle, no body, no trace of either leaving the restaurant parking lot.

The lack of clues surrounding Serena's disappearance only ramped up my frustration over Auntie O's informationless foretellings. Why hadn't she just listened to me? I needed her help. She'd left me in a position where I'd have to reach out to other witches whether I wanted to or not.

Tracking down the other two women proved equally fruitless. I could turn up only three things they had in common with Serena: they were women, they were supernaturals of some sort, and they were attending institutes of higher learning.

But they weren't even majoring in the same subjects. Heather, the young witch, was studying engineering; Willow, the born vampire, physics; and Serena business. As far as I could tell, they'd had no personal contact with each other.

Which left me firmly in square one.

Around eight thirty, I set my computer and my case

notebook aside and went for a long drive to clear my head. As if pulled there, my car took me on a winding route to the restaurant where Serena disappeared. I parked outside and watched the workers close up and leave one by one. Human, every single one, down to the night shift supervisor who cut off the lights and locked the doors. Though I was sore tempted to try the illumination spell again, I couldn't bring myself to defy Auntie O's dictate, not after inadvertently pushing her into a tizzy that afternoon.

I just needed some help, and I should've gone to someone else to get it. Anyone else, probably.

Oddly enough, that thought made the newly acquired cut on my inner wrist tingle and burn.

I rubbed a thumb over it, then tucked my hands in my lap and dropped my forehead to the steering wheel. Who could I ask about the illumination? Who could I trust to help me? I called up a handful of supernaturals outside the werewolf community and discarded them all, including my one quasi-friend who was also a witch. I sighed and put her back on the list as a possibility. If nothing else, she had a good ear for scuttlebutt.

I wasn't desperate enough to beg anyone else yet. Tomorrow, I'd hit the campus and visit Serena's classes, talk to her professors, maybe reach out to some of her classmates to see if they'd noticed anything unusual about her behavior, anything out of place.

And if that didn't work? I rubbed my wrist again. Yeah, I had a few last resorts up my sleeve, but I was a long way from wanting to use them.

I got home around ten and went straight to bed. Tomorrow was a workday, after all, and I had regular office hours to keep.

Sleep wasn't so easy to come by. The case went 'round and 'round in my mind, chasing its own tail like a puppy. I reviewed the details one by one, considered and discarded various actions, and slept fitfully with the missing young women ever in the forefront of my thoughts.

A light breeze brushed over the bed, waking me abruptly. I glanced at the alarm clock on the nightstand next to my bed and groaned at the bright red numbers. Just after midnight.

The curtains covering the window next to my bed lifted on another breeze, and I froze. I'd checked the windows during my nightly pre-bed routine. They'd all been locked, in every room. So how the hell had that one gotten open?

Slowly, I slipped a hand to the nightstand and the handgun holstered between it and the bed. Yes, I kept a gun beside my bed. Crossville is quiet, but it has its share of the criminal element. Being a former cop made me a target, on top of the heightened danger I faced just for being short and having boobs instead of a dick. Throw in the supernatural element, and yeah. Guns were a good backup.

Obviously, whoever had broken into my apartment had not considered that I was ready, willing, and able to punch an inconvenient and bloody hole in their body.

My night vision had adjusted enough to pick out a darkened shape standing near the end of my bed. My heart leapt once, then the cool detachment I'd developed as a cop kicked in. I aimed the nasty end of my gun at the shadow, but before I could act, a familiar voice spoke.

"A gun?" Dimitri said.

I reached over and flipped on the lamp sitting beside the traitorous alarm clock. Light flooded the area around the nightstand, just bright enough to make me squint. "What the hell are you doing breaking into my apartment?"

His lips twitched as if he were going to smile. "How else could I come to your aid when you called?"

"First off, I didn't call you. Secondly, you could try using the door like a normal person."

"Why be normal?"

If he hadn't said that with a straight face, I would've sworn he was teasing me.

I slipped my gun into its holster and sat up, smoothing my

hair away from my face with one hand as I pulled the covers up to my waist with the other. "Normal has a lot going for it. Like not getting you shot."

He hummed under his breath and stepped more fully into the light, out of the shadows. His hair was damp and wavy, and his outfit was similar to the one he'd worn Friday to Kinley's. Long-sleeved shirt, deep red this time, tucked into well-fitted jeans. I hid the automatic jump of attraction behind a sigh. Vampires have that effect on everyone, I reminded myself. Don't take it personally.

"Did you call to discuss your mother's disappearance?" he said.

"I didn't call you. And no, I don't want to talk about her."

In a flash, he was beside me holding my wrist. One thumb brushed over the tiny cut he'd inflicted on me a few days ago, and it throbbed once under his touch. "Liar."

Well, damn. I guess he had me there. "If I'd known all I had to do was touch it—"

His husky laugh cut me off. "It takes more than a simple touch. You needed me?"

Not him, specifically, but since he was here, I'd be a fool not to ask him about the recent disappearances. "I'm looking for a young woman."

"The missing she-wolf."

"What do you know?"

"Only that the Crossville pack is desperate to find her."

I narrowed my eyes at him. "That's really all you know?"

"Why would I lie?"

Why wouldn't he? I kept that thought where it belonged, in my head. Instead, I tugged gently on my wrist. "Let go."

"What have you discovered about your mother?"

"Nothing." Nothing I wanted to share with him, anyway. "Liar."

I scowled at him. "If you keep calling me a liar, I'm going to use that gun on you."

"Interesting." He let go of my wrist and stepped back into

the shadows at the foot of my bed, where the lamp's light didn't quite reach. "I have something for you."

"What, another bite?"

His expression turned savage. "Have a care, little witch."

I opened my mouth on a sharp retort, and sucked in a breath instead. Between one blink and the next, Dimitri had disappeared. Fear shivered down my spine. My God, he was fast, even for a vampire. He must be...

I stared bleakly at the window as the answer slowly came to me. Old. Very, very old.

And an old vampire was so much more dangerous than a new one. True, newly made vampires had no control over their thirst for blood. An old vampire, an experienced one, possessed the control, but the years eroded the one trait that newer vampires used to dampen their bloodlust: their humanity. New vampires were predictable, slower, still human enough to empathize with their prey.

An old vampire had no empathy.

I shivered again and forced myself out of bed and to the window. He'd warned me. That should've comforted me.

I closed the window and locked it, then climbed back into bed, one hand on my gun. I left the lamp on, too, as if it could protect me from him. As if the light alone could stave off the hunger I'd seen in Dimitri's dark, terrifying gaze.

ELEVEN

My phone's insistent ringing woke me. I was lying facedown on my bed with one hand still firmly attached to my gun and the other stuffed awkwardly beneath me. Slowly, I eased my wooden fingers off the weapon and pushed myself upright, groaning at the stiff muscles in my arms, shoulders, and back.

If I ever saw that vampire again, I wouldn't just shoot him. I'd shove garlic down his throat, drive a stake through his heart, and bury him upside down in consecrated ground. If he really pissed me off, I'd pour concrete over his grave, just to make sure he stayed there.

The ringing stopped as I flopped onto my side. I squinted at the alarm clock and stifled a curse. 4:37. My alarm didn't go off until seven sharp, which meant someone had woken me a good two hours and twenty-three minutes before they had to. Two hours and twenty-three minutes was a lot of sleeping time when you hadn't dozed off until well after midnight.

I shoved the covers off my legs and sat up. Yeah, I was definitely going to invest in some concrete, maybe that quick set stuff sold down at the hardware store. Right after I took a shower and downed half a gallon of coffee.

My phone started ringing again and, resigned, I picked it up and checked the number. A round bubble filled with Seth's face appeared above his name and number. I thumbed into the call and said, "Yeah?"

"We've got a problem. Are you dressed?"

"Not yet. What's the problem?"

"Another missing pack member."

I pinched the bridge of my nose, attempting to focus around the grit filling my brain. "Where are you?"

"On my way. Be ready when I get there."

The connection cut before I could say yea or nay. I set my phone on the nightstand, trudged toward the front door, and stuck a note for Seth on the outside before locking it again. Missing werewolf or no, I wasn't going anywhere without a shower and some coffee. Seth would just have to wait.

Fifteen minutes later, I walked out of my bedroom fully dressed, my hair pulled into a ponytail. Seth was in my living room, pacing between the front door and the kitchen in the narrow path bracketed by a bookcase and the end of my couch.

Did no one respect the locks on my doors and windows?

"You're going to wear a hole in my carpet," I said mildly. "The landlord won't like that."

He stopped dead in his tracks and turned a look on me that I couldn't interpret. Not angry, not startled, just a *look*.

I sighed and didn't bother mentioning that if I'd been less alert, I would've shot him instead of considering that the person walking in my living room was one of the few people who had a key to the front door.

"Vampire's been in here," he said.

Guilty as charged. Except Dimitri was an uninvited guest and I was not explaining that to Seth.

"Oh?" I overshot bright and perky, but it got the point across. I might as well have said *mind your own business.*

Seth took the hint, though he didn't look happy about it. "Ready?"

I bit back the urge to snap *no* at him. "Do we have time for coffee?"

"We can pick some up on the way."

Great. Convenience store coffee. Just what I needed after a mostly sleepless night.

He gave me that look again, then said, "I need you to do your witch thing."

I blinked at him, not sure I'd heard right. "My witch thing?"

"The thing you do with the chalk."

Oh. Right. My witch thing. "Sure. It's down in my office." Where I'd left everything after working the illumination spell at the scene of Serena's disappearance. Which did not matter. Gah. My brain needed to wake up.

I shook my head as I grabbed my keys, purse, and jacket, and led a brooding Seth down the inside stairs to my office. Witchy kit grabbed, I followed him outside to his truck, locking pertinent doors as we went.

True to his word, Seth stopped at a convenience store and bought large coffees and half a dozen biscuits filled with a variety of breakfast meats, which we heated in the in-store microwave. He handed a coffee and two biscuits off to me, then ate one-handed while he zigzagged through Crossville across the river into a bordering, unincorporated community.

I didn't bother chitchatting while eating, and Seth reciprocated, leaving the Tundra's cab quiet aside from the noise of occasional vehicles. It was too early for most commuters, way too early for school buses and soccer moms. The quiet soothed my grumpies away faster than listening to a radio would've.

By the time we reached a well-maintained park in the dead center of a middle-class neighborhood, I was awake enough to appreciate the approaching dawn. Not awake enough to appreciate spotting Mariah waiting for us on a sidewalk, but I took what I could get.

Seth parked behind her twenty-plus year old Bronco, and

we both slid out of the truck into the predawn chill and met her there, me ignoring the icy gaze she turned on me.

"Fill her in," Seth said gruffly.

"New wolf out jogging." Mariah nodded to the foot trail veering off the sidewalk into the park. "Went in here. Never came out."

Gee. She was a regular fount of information.

"Where does her trail end?" I said.

Mariah and Seth glanced at each other, then she said, "Why did you say *her*?"

"Because Serena is a female and two other female supernaturals have gone missing in the Greater Atlanta area."

"How do you know?"

I bit back my rising temper. What was it about her that irritated me so much?

"Because it's my job," I said bluntly. "Male or female?"

"Male."

There went one of the commonalities. "Show me."

Mariah glanced at Seth again, asking permission in that silent way they had, then turned toward the park. I snagged my witchy kit and followed her, with Seth close behind me shining a flashlight on the trail for my benefit. Depending on how far into the park we went, it might be dark and empty enough for me to cast my puny spell now instead of having to come back after sunset. It would be nice if I could avoid rubbing elbows with the junkies and thieves that probably used the park as a place of business for the night.

I spotted a heart carved into a tree trunk and revised my list of people I wanted to avoid. People having sex in the park after dark. Nature sex is prickly and dirty. Plus, at this time of year, just before the average date of our first frost, the temperature wasn't exactly comfortable at night. The whole setting was entirely unromantic. Don't believe anyone who tells you otherwise.

The trail skirted a playground, then wound through widely planted trees around the perimeter of the park. I asked questions as we walked, teasing information out of Seth and Mariah. The missing werewolf's name was William Thomas, aka Billy. He was twenty-three, five nine, of mixed race, and gaunt from his time in the cage.

I winced when Seth let that slip. If Billy had been confined after being turned, it was likely because he'd had a rough transition or couldn't control the change, probably both. I didn't know exactly what happened. That was strictly werewolf business. But I did know that no one talked about the cage, not being in one, not the level of control needed to get out, nothing. It was a closely guarded secret precisely because it was so personal.

No one liked to admit that they couldn't control themselves, especially when losing control could turn you into a rabid serial killer.

About ten minutes out, Mariah turned toward the park's center, into a more densely wooded area where the sparse grass gave way to a tangle of undergrowth. The trail narrowed here and was covered by a thick layer of fallen leaves that crackled softly under every footstep. Oak, poplar, hickory. I only recognized a few, and mostly from what I could see of the trees themselves, not the leaves.

This part of the park's trail seemed less well-used. As we walked deeper into the copse, it was easy to see why. Yellow-leaved brambles snagged my jeans and acorns crunched underfoot. Not exactly jogger friendly. I couldn't see suburban parents allowing their children to play in the wilder area, either, though it couldn't have been more than a couple of acres in size.

But it was just big enough to support a tiny clearing near the center, and that's where Mariah stopped. She knelt beside a ring of stones surrounding blackened wood, touched a finger to the charcoal, and lifted it to her nose.

While she was using her sniffing superpower, I borrowed the flashlight from Seth and circled around her, searching for footprints, blood, signs of a struggle, anything to indicate what might've happened to Billy Thomas. The leaves here had been churned up, though not enough to clear the ground of detritus. Other than that, I couldn't spot a single clue, not even a broken twig or branch.

But it was still a little dark out.

Mariah stood and turned toward the trail. I followed her gaze as Seth moved aside and a waif-like early twenty-something young woman stepped into the clearing beside him. Her white-blonde hair was cut in a pixie style, and she wore a drab green explorer's jacket over slim fitted jeans.

Unless I'd missed the mark, she was also entirely human.

Seth played the flashlight over her, and she turned wideset eyes on him. "Did you find Billy?"

"Not yet," Seth said.

I stepped forward, hand out. "I'm Vanessa Kinley, a private investigator. Seth hired me to find Billy."

Mariah snorted softly as the young woman took my hand in her fine-boned one and said, "Shelly Fisher." She dropped my hand, and her nose reddened at the tip. "Billy's girlfriend. We were supposed to meet out here last night. He said he wanted to show me something."

Her voice lifted at the end in a soft question. I looked at Seth, but his gaze was fixed on the ground behind a nearby tree.

"About what time?" I asked Shelly.

She tucked her hands into the jackets pockets and rolled her slim shoulders. "Two ish? I asked him why we had to wait until the middle of the night, and he just laughed kinda hard. Like he wasn't sure how to explain, you know?"

I had a feeling she'd hit the nail on the head there. "Do you have any idea what he wanted to show you?"

She shook her head and muttered a soft *nunh-unh.*

"How long have you been dating?"

"Since high school off and on. He was in the Army for a coupla years, then..."

"Yes?" I prompted.

"When he came back, he was different. Harder. But he said he still loved me and wanted to be with me. Except one day, he just disappeared. Sent me a letter saying he had to go out of town for a while, he'd see me soon. Wait for him, he said." She sniffed and swiped a tear off her cheek. "I was like, why should I wait, you know? Guy keeps disappearing. But he writes me another letter and another, and then he turns up outta the blue saying he's got something to show me, and now he's gone again."

Yeah, I wouldn't stick around if a guy had dicked around with me like that. Not sure what that said about either one of us, though. Behind me, Seth and Mariah were moving around, rustling the clearing's undergrowth. I shifted so that all three of them were in my field of view, and kept one eye on the werewolves while questioning Shelly.

"What time did you get here?" I said.

"About five 'til two. Had to sneak out." Her laugh was half humor, half sob. She swiped another tear away. "I hate living with my folks, but until I get out of school, it's that or a dorm room. Cheaper to live at home, you know? And Billy said once he—"

Seth's low curse interrupted whatever she was going to confess. "Clothes."

I touched Shelly's elbow. "Stay right here, ok?"

She nodded, and I picked my way across the clearing to where Seth and Mariah were standing. They were both staring down at the ground where a large, moss-covered rock had been overturned. While we'd been talking, the sun had gently risen, casting enough light for me to make out the hole dug into the red clay dirt beneath the rock and the pile of clothes filling it.

"Billy's," Mariah said.

I glanced around to make sure Shelly had stayed put on the other side of the clearing, then said softly, "What else?"

"Strange magic."

"Coming from the clothes?"

"And the fire."

"Did Billy put his clothes there or someone else?"

She turned a speculative look on me. "Can't tell."

I hummed under my breath. "Why not burn the clothes?"

"Maybe to make it look like Billy did it?"

Seth shook his head. "No, he would've put them somewhere safe. Somewhere clean."

I caught his meaning. If Billy intended to change in front of his girlfriend, he'd want his clothes to be wearable once he was human again. It made sense, but it still didn't tell us who'd put Billy's clothes under a rock or why. Might rule out a supernatural, though. Surely most supes knew the basics about werewolf clothing etiquette.

I had another question. "How did y'all find out Billy was missing?"

Seth's gaze turned toward Shelly, and I turned with it, then walked across the clearing toward her.

"What did you do when Billy didn't show?" I said as I approached.

Her gaze leapt between me and the two wolves like a rabbit trapped between predators. "I waited for a while," she stammered out.

"How long?"

"Ten minutes maybe? It was dark and the woods creep me out, and the longer I was out here..." She swallowed hard and her gaze darted between us again. "I got spooked, ok? So I ran back to the car and locked myself inside and called Mr. Rhone."

"Why him? Why not the police?"

"Billy said if anything ever happened to him..."

Her voice trailed off as Seth walked up to us, but I got her gist. Billy had covered at least one of his bases, which proved he wasn't as dumb as he seemed. Showing his girlfriend the change in the middle of a suburban park at two a.m.? I shook my head. I was only half a decade older than him, but it made me wonder if I'd ever been that dumb.

Then I remembered the rune and Auntie's warnings against using magic and hid a wince. Yeah, I had.

I attempted a smile for Shelly's benefit and said to Seth, "I've got what I need. Maybe you could see Shelly home?"

It was a huge hint for him to get the human out of the way so I could do my witchy thing. Thankfully, he took it. I watched the two of them walk away from the clearing along the narrow trail, then turned back to the fire ring where Billy Thomas's trail had disappeared.

TWELVE

I asked Mariah to keep an ear out for intruders. Unlikely at just shy of dawn, but possible. Suburbanites loved their early morning jogs.

Meanwhile, I turned my attention to the fire ring and the embers touched by what Mariah had called strange magic. Drawing a chalk circle in the dirt was challenging, though not impossible. It didn't have to be perfect or unbroken, merely containing in my mind. Or that's what worked for me. Maybe I was doing it wrong.

I shrugged off the doubt instilled by Auntie's shrill disbelief. Second guessing the process was not going to help me find Billy. It wasn't going to help me call forth the magic and mold it.

I squatted and etched the rune onto a nice sized piece of charred wood within the circle of stone, then placed my hand over it and concentrated. Billy. Transformation. His werewolf nature. Not much to go on, but I'd made do with less.

A shimmering pink glow emanated from under my hand and spilled out, filling the circle. Amorphous, undefined. I concentrated harder, hoping to refine the magic, and finally, it coalesced into the figure of a young, slender man squatting beside the fire. Head, shoulders and arms, midthigh forward to knees. The rest of him was cut off. I frowned. Hadn't made the circle big enough.

The young man's head turned and he started to rise, then he was pulled out of the circle by an unseen force, like a yoyo yanked backward. Just as the image shimmered out of existence, a head popped up, hovering three feet or so over the center of the fire ring.

My brother's face.

This time, I didn't pull away the way I had when Mom's image appeared. I wanted more, needed the details the lingering magic might render. A moment later, the image blinked out and disappeared, its end a byproduct of my lack of talent, but I'd seen enough. Nick's face was definitely not part of Billy's reality. But what was it doing in the illumination? How had it gotten there?

Slowly, I withdrew my hand and brushed my palm along my thigh, rubbing off the chalk and ember residue. The leaves rustled beside me, and I looked up. Mariah was standing beside me, her stance rigid.

"How long have you known?" she barked out.

I retrieved the water bottle and squirted water over the rune, then stood and rubbed a foot across the rough chalk circle, breaking it. "Known what?"

"That your brother is part of this."

I glanced at her, startled. "What?"

"This. The disappearances."

"The..."

"I saw his image there, in your magic."

My eyes went wide. "You saw that?"

Her expression blanked. "It was hard to miss. How long have you known about him?"

Slowly, it dawned on me what she meant, and my heart tightened with the first glimmer of fear. "You think he's responsible for Billy's disappearance? That's crazy! Nick wouldn't harm a fly."

"I saw him," she said, each word low and angry. "I told Seth not to trust you."

She spat in the dirt and said, "Witches," then spun and loped out of the clearing at a rapid clip, her long strides eating up the distance.

"Wait!" I yelled, but she was already gone. Damn werewolves. Even in their human forms, they were fast, too fast for a runt like me to keep up with. I ran after her anyway. I didn't know why Nick's image had appeared within the illumination, just as I didn't know why Mom's had, but I knew one thing for certain: Nick was not responsible for the missing supernaturals.

By the time I reached the street, the sun had popped over the horizon, and I was sweaty and pissed. Mariah's Bronco was gone. Seeing the empty spot where she'd parked reminded me of three crucial pieces of information: Seth had followed Shelly home; I'd left my cellphone at home in my rush to get out the door that morning; and my wallet was in Seth's truck.

I rubbed the heel of my palm against my forehead, then set off to find an open business. Screw my lack of a ride. I had to warn Nick. Unless I was sorely mistaken, Mariah was on her way to his apartment right now. The last thing he needed was a pissed off werewolf showing up unannounced on his doorstep.

I found a convenience store a few blocks away and conned the clerk into letting me borrow her phone. Nick didn't answer, not the first time I called, nor the second. I left a message the third time, thanked the clerk, and walked out with my witchy kit in hand.

Then I pointed myself toward home and started walking.

Seth pulled up beside me before I got too far. I stopped on the sidewalk as he reached across the seat and opened the passenger's side door for me from the inside.

"Nick didn't do it," I said. "He's got an alibi for one of the disappearances, maybe more. We have to pin down the times and match them to Nick's schedule."

His expression didn't change. "Get in, Nessie."

"He didn't do it."

I hated the edge of desperation underscoring my words, hated that fatigue had weakened my control and reduced me to pleading, hated the hope that Seth would listen to me, and the knowledge that nothing I said would outweigh whatever Mariah had told him.

"Get in," he gritted out, and my hope sank like a stone in water.

I got in. Buckled up. Clutched the witchy kit in my lap as if it were a lifeline, and tried not to let the fear clogging my throat choke me during the drive home.

Mariah stood outside Nick's apartment door, her back to the wall. Her gaze held a trace of hard defiance and the seething boil of anger.

"What are you going to do to him?" I asked Seth.

"Watch him," he replied. "Nick's on lockdown until we get to the bottom of this."

I swallowed the urge to defend him again. That was a waste of time. Better to devote myself to finding the real culprit behind the disappearances, starting with why and how Mom and Nick's images had appeared in the illuminations.

Seth followed me into my apartment and closed the door behind us.

I dropped my keys, wallet, and witchy kit onto the cabinet holding the TV and snapped, "Am I under suspicion, too?"

"Nessie..."

I rounded on him, suddenly so mad I could've hit him. "You know Nick. He's your friend. You've spent time with him, so much time you should know he would never, ever hurt Serena or any of the other wolves."

"We have to be sure," Seth began, and I laughed. The hard bitterness of it surprised us both. Seeing that startled surprise on his expression helped me pull back on the helpless rage simmering within me, but only just.

"He has an ironclad alibi for at least one of the kidnappings," I said quietly. "You know that. Mariah knows that. And yet you're holding him anyway."

"We don't have another lead." When I started to retort, Seth held up a hand. "This is what we have, Nessie. I have to protect my pack, and if that means keeping an eye on Nick, then so bet it. It's for his protection, too."

I barked out another laugh. "His protection. Don't even try to pull that on me, Seth. Don't. Even."

"Nessie—"

"You don't get to call me that," I hissed, then I turned on a heel and headed toward my bathroom and a hot shower. Let Seth find his own way out. I was tired and sticky and needed to think.

THIRTEEN

I got out of the shower with a half-baked plan outlined. Once dressed, I concealed my Glock 27 in a holster at the small of my back, beneath my sweater, pulled on comfortable boots, and grabbed a matching jacket on my way out of my bedroom. Seth was gone, thank God. No idea what I would've done if he'd still been there, but it wouldn't have been pretty for either one of us.

I had bigger fish to fry anyway, or meaner ones. As I grabbed my keys, wallet, and cellphone (wasn't forgetting it this time, damn it), I mentally girded my loins in preparation for a confrontation with Mariah.

But when I stepped out of the apartment, the hallway was empty. Wary, I locked my door, then tapped on Nick's across the hallway. A moment later, the locks clicked open and his sleepy face appeared in a crack between the door and doorframe.

"Izzit?" he said.

I shook my head, unsure where to start. Finally, I blurted out, "Have you talked to Seth?"

"Yeah." He rubbed a hand over his face, failing to hide his frown. "Don't worry about it. I'll be ok."

"That's not the point. He has no right to do this to you."

"You'd do the same in his shoes."

I opened my mouth on a protest and closed it again. "Not the point."

"Sure, it is. Anyway, they're not keeping me from doing anything I need to do."

"Yeah, anything except move around without a werewolf shadowing your every move. He put Mariah on you."

Nick hooked a thumb over his shoulder, toward the room behind him. "I know. She's making coffee right now."

I gaped at him. "You let her in? Are you out of your mind? She's a *werewolf*."

"I've seen her change, so yeah, kinda obvious, Nessie, and..." A yawn interrupted whatever he was going to say. He hid it against the back of the door, then said, "They're just keeping an eye on me, that's all. Nothing to worry about."

Nothing to worry about? Had sleep robbed him of his senses?

"I know that look," he added. "Seth explained everything. Now go figure out who did this and don't worry about me. Ok?"

"Sure," I hissed. "I'll just go do that, since you've let a man-eating werewolf into your apartment."

He snorted out a tired laugh and closed the door on me, and I stared blankly at it. He'd let his guard into his apartment, a woman who made her living tracking down people who harmed the pack, then brought them to justice in the brutally vicious way of the wolf. I sure hoped he knew what he was doing, but a funny feeling in my gut insisted that he'd only made things worse.

Peterson was waiting on the sidewalk outside my office, leaning against a Victorian-style lamppost like a clichéd version of a noir detective.

Which is what I got for using the outside stairs.

"Run out of donuts?" I said as I stepped onto the sidewalk and turned toward my office entrance.

"I'm waiting for the Hot Now sign to light up. What happened to William Thomas?"

"Who?"

"Missing werewolf. Disappeared last night around two a.m. One of Seth Rhone's werewolves. Second one in a weekend."

"There you go spouting craziness again. I suggest meds."

"Got 'em. Didn't help."

He pushed away from the lamppost and stepped close, pushing into my personal space.

I spun around and headed toward the parking garage. Screw it. My eyes were gritty, my jaw hurt from clenching my teeth together in frustration and worry and...stuff. I didn't need Peterson wearing me down, looking for answers I couldn't give him.

Behind me, Peterson said, "You have to talk to me sometime, Kinley."

I waved a hand at him without turning around. No, I didn't, not if I could help it.

The Crossville Community College campus was just warming up when I got there, which was more than I could say for the air. Mist hung over the grounds, resisting the sun's energy as it rose above the skyline, curling around trees dressed in the brilliant reds and yellows of fall.

Students strolled along the sidewalks, backpacks slung over sweatshirts and jackets, some human, some not. A male supernatural of indeterminate origins bounced down the steps to the admin building and brushed past me. Something about him seemed familiar, his build, the color of his hair, but my tired brain couldn't quite place him. Probably a teacher whose picture I'd seen when I'd started investigating Serena's college life, or maybe one of Kinley's customers.

The thought of my brother's bar knocked my brain into some semblance of focus, reminding me of the urgency of this case. I hurried up the steps and through the entrance, then searched until I found someone to help me. Fifteen minutes later, I had directions to where Serena's classes were being held and a rough idea of the campus bus schedule.

I'd missed the day's first class, so I headed toward the second class by way of the student center serving as the campus's central hub. The student center was three stories of student-oriented madness cut into a hill with the main entrance to the top two stories on one side and the entrance to the basement-level floor on the other.

My approach was toward the main entrance and the ground, or middle, floor, which held a mall style food court with restaurant vendors running along two curved walls and seating in the center. The seating was a mix of dining tables and chairs, and large sofas placed around low-lying tables. Two large screen TVs were mounted on the far wall, bracketing the back exit, both turned to morning news programs. Signs pointed toward stairs leading to the lowest floor's gym and health center and the upper floor's bookstore and study areas.

I headed through a tiled foyer past a bulletin board toward a chain restaurant and ordered a breakfast burrito and coffee to go. The cashier who took my order didn't recognize Serena's picture, but as he put it, "a lot of kids pass through here." It was difficult to remember every face unless you had a class with someone.

I ate standing up with a shoulder propped against one wall while scanning the students moving through the open space. It was a typical crowd. Lots of shining faces, lots of hopes and dreams visible in sleepy smiles and bright eyes. I'd gone to the University of Georgia in Athens a couple of hours east of Crossville rather than staying at home. It had been another way of escaping the damage Mom did when she left, another way of rebelling. Just like police work. Just like the rune I'd torn out of a grimoire.

Not every rebellion ended badly. I'd gotten a job I'd loved doing work that was important to me, and the magic had helped me solve cases no one else could. And I was still doing that. Only now, the stakes were so much more personal than they'd been when I was a rookie cop thumbing my nose at Mom's memory.

When I finished eating, I threw my wrapper away and pulled out my phone, then went from table to table showing Serena's picture around. A few students remembered her from a class they'd taken together. I took their names and contact information down and moved on. No one seemed to know she was missing, and after fifteen minutes spent circulating through the room, I hadn't met a single student who had a current class with her.

By the time I'd made the rounds, it was almost time for the second class to start. I walked out the way I'd entered, past the bulletin board. On impulse, I stopped and looked through the flyers and notes tacked to the large corkboard. Roommates needed. Tutors offering their services. Job fairs, concerts, lectures by guest speakers.

I homed in on the word "solar" typed onto a flyer nearly covered by a bright poster spelling out student rights and an advertisement for a local laundromat. When I shifted the covering papers aside, I discovered an announcement for a lecture given two weeks prior by a visiting astrophysicist. The lecture was titled "Goldilocks: Habitable Extrasolar Planets."

Serena had a telescope in the corner of her room.

I took a picture of the flyer, then hurried out the door to what should've been Serena's second class of the day.

FOURTEEN

The morning dragged as I made the rounds of Serena's classes, chatting with teachers and classmates, trying to find some clue as to who might've been behind her disappearance. Word was beginning to get around. She'd missed soccer practice over the weekend, missed her first class that day, and as the absences piled up, the students who knew her began to express concern.

By the time I hit the fourth class, my eyes were crossing from a combination of business jargon and a lack of sleep. This one covered something about investment management, and it was, quite simply, incomprehensible.

What? I'd gone into criminal justice for a reason. Business was Nick's field. If he hadn't been under lockdown, I would've made him come sit through these lectures.

I shoved down the bitterness at that thought and stood with the rest of the class, thankful it was over. I'd cleared my sitting in with the professor first, but the students had shot me funny looks throughout. Maybe the rumor mill had already reached them as to why I was on campus asking questions about their classmate. Or maybe they were, like humans everywhere, curious about the stranger in their midst.

Whatever it was, this time two students approached me as the class ended, both female, both wearing their straight, dark brown hair down around their shoulders.

"We heard you were a cop," one said. She was five four and wore a loose Falcons sweatshirt over black leggings. A dimple winked in one cheek as she spoke.

"Private investigator. Vanessa Kinley." Obligingly, I pulled out my license and handed them business cards. "Do you know Serena Jimenez?"

The young women exchanged glances, then the second one spoke. She was taller, slimmer, more athletic under the bright red sweater tunic she wore over skinny jeans.

"Yeah. I play soccer with her. We're both business majors, so we've got a lot of classes together."

"When did you last see her?" I said.

"Friday," the second young woman said promptly. "Here on campus. We had a late class that day. She had to go pick up supper for her family, then we were going to study. Exams."

"Yeah," the first young woman added. "We had a game on Saturday and plans for that night. It's not like her to no show."

That's the impression I'd gotten. I jotted down their names (dimpled Cassidy and serious Dulce) and numbers in my notes and deflected their not-so-subtle hints for me to feed them information. They were about to hurry off to another class when another question popped into my head.

"Hey," I said as they passed by me on their way to the exit. "What kind of plans did you have with Serena on Saturday?"

Cassidy rolled her eyes. "Looking at stars. Serena's nuts about her telescope."

"So it was a regular thing?"

"Yeah, sure. Especially since she dragged us to that first lecture. What was it?"

"Alien life," Dulce said. "This week's a repeat, but in depth."

"Wait, it's a lecture series?" I said.

"Oh, yeah. Professor from Tech or somewhere." Cassidy flipped her hair over her shoulder on another eye roll. "Serena made a bunch of us go with her. I mean, it's interesting and all, but who makes money as an astronomer?"

I buttoned away a comment about the multi-billion-dollar space industry and thanked them for their time. The lecture series seemed like a promising lead, if only because it introduced a stranger into the mix. I made a note to follow up on it, then girded my metaphorical loins and headed off to try to catch the professors or teaching assistants for classes five and six.

As much as I would've liked to stay on campus indefinitely, questioning students as they came and went, my energy flagged as the morning wore on. By the end of the sixth class, I was more than ready to call it quits. How the hell did students keep up with that kind of schedule? Granted, not all classes were held every day, but still. I was pooped.

No one had anything new to add anyway. Serena was a model student, well-liked, hard working. People were concerned by her absence. I had nothing to say that would ease that concern.

My eyes were gritty and I could barely take a step without yawning. Still, I had one more person I wanted to speak to.

On the way home, I detoured to the wrong side of the tracks and parked at a rundown strip mall housing a fortune teller's shop run by Angel Miller, aka Madame Cassandra. It was the only active business left there, the only one people visited.

Maybe because Angel was good at her job, even if she was a con artist. As a kitchen witch, she had about as much divining ability in her as I did, but she was good at reading people and good at keeping her ears open. She'd helped me out before, more than once, most recently during an arson investigation. Thinking about that investigation brought the anger bubbling back. That investigation had been conducted on Seth's behalf, when someone torched part of one of his housing developments. Without me, we would never have found the person responsible.

Boy, gratitude didn't last long anymore, did it?

With a tight shake of my head, I cut my car's engine off and got out. I hated to tap her again so soon, but needs must. The shop was closed tight, but it was a school day, so Angel might be in there anyway, cleaning or prepping for the night ahead. I banged on the front door, felt the plate glass rattle under my hand. Heard nothing from inside.

Frowning, I banged again, and when that didn't produce results, walked around the side of the building to the back. Angel's white Chevy Spark was nowhere to be seen.

Ok, Plan B.

I got back in my car and drove to a less seedy area of Crossville, a neighborhood much like the Jimenez's, full of tidy houses on small lots and signs reading *children at play.* Angel's home was in the middle of the street, a white shotgun house with cheery blue trim surrounded by a metal chain link fence. Roses, jasmine, and trumpet vines spilled over the fence and crawled up bird feeders and trellises. Late blooming gardenias filled the air with their rich perfume and the hint of a garden peeked through the open-ended carport from the back yard.

There sat her Spark, filling the carport. I parked as close to the curb as I could, then got out and pushed through the fence to the front door. The doorbell buzzed loud enough to hear from the concrete bottomed porch. I stuffed my hands in the front pockets of my jeans and tried to suppress a yawn. Damn, I was tired.

A curtain fluttered to my right behind a row of windows. Angel didn't come to the door, though, so after a minute, I rang the doorbell again.

Finally, the door opened a mere two inches, just wide enough to catch the hank of bleached white hair falling around her face. "Are you crazy?" Angela hissed. "Go away before somebody sees you."

Nonplussed, I stared at her. We'd always been on good terms, even though we weren't always on the same side of the law. Truth be told, I liked Angel and her crazy Madame

Cassandra persona. She had a good heart and was a great mom.

I liked her even better when she fed me information on the sly.

She started to close the door, and I slapped a palm to it, hoping to hold her off long enough to get something out of her.

"What's going on, Angel?" I said. "What have you heard?"

"Nothing. I haven't heard anything."

"Yeah, that's why you're hiding inside your house instead of talking to me like a civilized witch."

"Who said I was civilized?"

I sighed. This was not getting me anywhere. "Look. I need help. Werewolves are going missing—"

"Not just werewolves," she muttered.

"Exactly," I countered. "So you should really help a witch out and tell me what you know."

She closed her eyes and rested her forehead against the edge of the door. "I can't talk to you, Nessa. You can't be here."

"Angel, come on."

"Just go before you put my kids in danger."

That surprised me so much the muscles in my arm went limp. My hand slid down the door and she closed it quietly. The locks clicked into place, and that's when I realized what was wrong with this picture, part of it anyway.

Cartoons had been playing in the background. Angel's kids were home on a school day, when she made a point of having them in school every day no matter what was going on in their lives. "Short of blood," she'd told me once.

Like I said. She was a good mom.

I backed away, still caught on the way she'd evaded me. What could possibly be so wrong that just being seen with me put her and her kids in danger?

I shook my head, baffled by the conversation, by the whole damn situation. Something screwy was going on here, something I couldn't quite put my finger on. I wouldn't solve it by harassing Angel, though, but maybe I could find some other cages to rattle before things got too far away from me.

FIFTEEN

I dragged myself into the bar half an hour later. If the situation had been different, I would've gone straight to bed, but I couldn't not check on my dingbat brother. You know, the one who let the big bad wolf inside his apartment.

Was Mariah's wolf even potty trained?

I spotted her sitting at the wooden bar across Kinley's as soon as I walked in, and man, was I tempted to ask her. Pretty sure she'd kick my ass from here to Sunday, but what the hell. Maybe I'd get some licks in, too.

Nick the Dingbat was standing behind the bar drying glasses fresh out of the commercial dishwasher located in the kitchen. He winked at me like a hundred- and twenty-pound werewolf wasn't sitting six feet away from him. Ok, she was in her human form, but that did nothing to diminish her deadliness.

Lunch customers filled the space between us. I plodded through them on my way toward Nick, nodding and smiling like a good sister, and finally managed to get myself there without stumbling, a sainted miracle. I was so tired, my skin tingled, and not in a good way. Not even in a magical way. More like the *if I don't get in bed soon I'm going to pass out where I stand* way.

I jerked my chin at Mariah as I approached my brother, and pitched my voice just loud enough to be heard over the music and conversations. "If she's going to take up space for a while, you should put her to work."

"I thought about it," he said.

"Do it. I'd love to see her face when you hand her a tub and have her bus tables."

Mariah turned her head toward me, away from the news program playing on the TV nearest her. I grinned at her, and yeah, it was just as mean and ugly as I felt. She was wasting her time tailing Nick. We all knew it.

"Cut it out, Nessie," Nick said.

"Nope."

I stood on tiptoe and bussed his cheek, then patted his shoulder and slipped through the door into the kitchen and the hallway beyond. A nap, a sandwich, another hot shower. That should do the trick, and if it didn't, well. I'd figure it out later, when my brain wasn't so fuzzy.

I was tempted to drop into bed without stripping down, but old habits die hard. Once I'd locked myself in, I dropped everything into its proper place as I headed toward my bedroom. Keys, wallet, cellphone, jacket, boots, and finally, I made it to the end of my bed with its simple sleigh frame and the steamer trunk sitting at the foot.

A thick book rested there, in the empty space between my workout clothes and my sleep t-shirt, a book I hadn't placed there.

Carefully, I reached out and flipped the thin, black cover open. Felt like leather. Pages flipped with it, and I was almost relieved to see evenly spaced handwriting scrawled around sketches of plants, animals, and symbols. Runes, too.

I flipped the cover closed and took a moment to ponder it. Where had it come from? How had it gotten—

Oh, right. Dimitri. He'd said something about having

something for me, but not what that something was. I hadn't thought to ask either, what with having a vampire drop into my apartment unannounced. This grimoire, I presumed, and on that thought, my worn-out brain hit a wall. I stripped the rest of my clothes off and dropped into bed naked, without another thought given to the mysterious book my unwanted vampire visitor had left behind.

A few hours later, after a decent nap and a shower and nightfall, I checked my messages and found one from Seth and two from clients. The first client message turned out to be nothing. The other was a signal I'd been waiting for.

Seth's text read *call me.* And since he hadn't specified why, I decided to wait until I was finished with my paying clients.

The signal? A possible cheating spouse. The husband, a stay-at-home dad, suspected his globetrotting CFO wife of having an affair. He couldn't afford my rates for travel (apparently, she'd put him on a strict budget), so he'd asked me to follow her while she was stateside.

I was happy to. Money was money, after all. But I'd warned him that if she was having an affair, she might be confining it to when she was out of town and away from prying eyes.

I gathered up my stuff, drove toward the wealthier side of town, and parked at a busy gas station across the street from their home. Well, across the street from the lone entrance to the gated community in which they lived. Gotta love those security conscious folks.

The view from the gas station, however, was amazing, especially now that it was full dark outside and the streetlights had come on. It was a clear shot from where I sat to the fully illuminated gate across the street. Mrs. CFO drove a shiny red Lexus sedan, the only one in the insular neighborhood. According to Mr. CFO, she had a habit of eating supper at home, then going back to work, a habit that had caused no end of strife and suspicion and had led directly to my being hired to follow her.

This was my first night on the case, not counting time spent digging into her background. She'd been in Japan negotiating quote *some kind of deal* unquote when Hubby hired me.

While waiting for her Lexus to appear, I opened my cellphone and read the astronomy lecture flyer with one eye on the gate. A minivan drove out, the gate shut behind it, and I went back to my phone. Dr. Sam Greely. No photo, no bio beyond "guest lecturer." Whoever had put the flyer together needed to work on their marketing skills. Me, I'd want to see some credentials.

I opened a browser and typed in the professor's name with my gaze firmly glued to the gate. Glanced down to see the result, and nothing. Damn it. The gate opened and a flash of red alerted me. Yup, there she was, the potential cheating spouse. Time for some real work.

I dropped my phone onto the passenger's seat, started my car, and pulled out two cars behind Mrs. CFO's easily tagged Lexus, with a mental note to follow up on Dr. Greely asap.

SIXTEEN

Mrs. CFO turned out to not be very exciting. I followed her to a CVS, wandered inside after her. Casually checked out her purchases before walking out again, my head buried in my cellphone like every other red-blooded American.

Toothpaste and toilet paper. Whoo, this woman was living the high life.

She went straight from there to her office. I stayed outside and waited. One thing I'd grilled Hubby on? Where her office was inside corporate. I'd already figured out where to sit so I could watch her office from the outside and estimated how long it would take her to get there. Right on cue, light flooded her office window. I settled in for a good wait, my mind blessedly empty.

An hour later, Mrs. CFO hadn't come out and I was getting antsy. Stakeouts had always been Peterson's thing, not mine. I was too restless on a normal day. Tonight, frustration had wound me into a tight little knot of stress.

I pushed aside the personal crap and focused on the window. Light on. Check. Mrs. CFO pacing back and forth, her solo shadow easily seen. Check.

My cellphone rang just as I was checking the grounds for security. I picked it up, saw Seth's name, and sighed. I'd forgotten to call him back.

I thumbed into the call and said, "Yeah?"

"We found a body."

I sat up, all thoughts of the missus gone. "A supe?"

Seth grunted, which I took as a yes. Because duh, why else would he be calling me?

"Where?" I said.

"Don't yell."

"I wasn't yelling. Why would I yell?"

"Because you yell when you're mad."

And werewolves are sensitive to sound. I ground my teeth together. "Just tell me."

"In the parking garage across from Kinley's."

A chill ran down my spine and my hand spasmed on my phone. I'd been in that parking garage not two hours ago. How the hell had I missed a dead body?

"Nessie," he said, then, "Vanessa. It was next to Nick's truck."

"No," I whispered hoarsely.

"We're trying to keep the police from finding out."

"I can be there..." My gaze flicked to Mrs. CFO's office. The window was dark. Damn it. I had to follow her. "I'm on a job."

"Fuck the job, Nessie."

I wished I could. "I'll be there as soon as I can."

A cold lump settled into my stomach. I cut the connection, dropped my phone onto the passenger's seat. Fifteen minutes, I promised myself. If Mrs. CFO hadn't settled somewhere in fifteen minutes, I was cutting her loose and driving back home.

Seth was right. Fuck the job. That body could only mean one thing: Someone was framing my brother. But the pack wouldn't buy the neatly tied package someone had dropped literally on our doorstep, no matter how convenient it was. They would want retribution, and their retribution was the kind that came at the end of claws and teeth.

Fuck the job, I thought again, especially when my brother's life was on the line.

Mrs. CFO drove to a hotel a couple of towns over. Not a cheap one, either. One with security and a mid-three figure price tag per night. I'd have to wheedle my way in and I didn't have time for that.

I watched her get out of her car and head toward the entrance, then slipped out of my car, camera in hand. Snap, snap, snap, and I had pictures of her entering the building and her car parked there. It would've been better if she'd made kissy kissy outside with some guy who wasn't her husband, but given the circumstances, this would have to do. I could track her down later. My brother needed me now.

Five minutes later, I was on the interstate headed back to Crossville, breaking every speed limit in sight and praying I didn't run across a state trooper. Local cops would cut me some slack. State troopers? Not a chance.

I made it back to Crossville in record time, though far later than I'd wanted to, and found an empty spot on the street outside the parking garage. Lucky for me. Kinley's did a steady business on Mondays during football season. And Nick should've been in there all evening under Mariah's beady little gaze, a rock-solid alibi.

Now if I could just convince Seth of that.

I kept my walk steady and purposeful as I entered the parking garage and headed toward Nick's usual parking spot. Assigned, because Seth wasn't a dick, even if he was being one right now. It was part and parcel of renting from him.

Seth was standing a dozen feet away from the end of Nick's truck, well away from the body still splayed across the concrete floor. Miles was there, and Jamal, and a werewolf I didn't recognize, probably because they were in wolf form.

The parking garage's overhead lights were plenty bright enough to see the damage as I approached and stopped beside Seth. Even from that distance, I could smell the stench of rotting flesh.

Not a fresh kill, then. If it was a kill at all.

Seth's gaze had snapped to me and followed my progress toward him. Now, he took my arm and escorted me closer, as if I'd never seen a dead body before and needed the support.

"We waited for you," he said.

His voice was low and gravelly. Miles's brow was furrowed, Jamal's expression stony, but the wolf emitted a rumbling growl, its lips curled back in a mild snarl.

"Keep it away from the body," I snapped, then I shrugged off Seth's hand and knelt.

It was a woman, young. Teens or early twenties was my guess. Forensics wasn't my thing, but you picked up a few things if you saw enough bodies, and I had. No blood under her that I could tell, not that it mattered. The stench was remarkably strong and mostly blocked out the faint aroma of what I thought might be dirt. She hadn't died here, hadn't bled here. Hadn't been here when I'd left a few hours ago. My parking spot was just a couple of spaces over. I would've seen her if she'd been here then.

Why had no one called it in? People came and went from this garage all the time. At night, it served as an overflow for visitors to the downtown area. Lots of Kinley's customers parked here.

So the body had to've been dumped here recently, which meant security footage from cameras mounted on the shops nearby.

But there was one more question I needed an answer to before I tackled that.

I stood and leveled a steady stare on Seth. "How did you know she was here?"

His jaw worked for a minute, then he said, "Anonymous call."

I barked out a short laugh. "Do you still think Nick is

responsible for the disappearances?"

"We can't rule out—"

I cut him off with a sweep of my hand, earning another growl from the wolf. "Was Mariah with him all evening?"

He glanced away, which was answer enough.

"Say it with me, Seth. Alibi. Come on. Say it."

"He's under the protection of the pack until this is cleared up."

"This," I said, pointing to the body, "should damn well clear it up."

"Nessie," he began, and I cut him off again.

"I told you not to call me that."

"We have to be sure."

"You mean you're under a shit ton of pressure from the pack to find a suspect and he's a convenient target. I thought you were his friend." I huffed out a breath and encompassed Miles and Jamal in my scornful gaze. "Oh, but I forgot. Pack comes first, right?"

Seth and his lieutenants met my gaze steadily, the bastards.

I dug my keys out of my pocket and tossed them to Miles. "Get my camera out of my car, will you? Make sure you take a good sniff of it. I wouldn't want to be accused of ferrying a dead body to help establish Nicky's alibi."

"Vanessa," Seth said, a warning growl underscoring the word.

"Fuck you, Mr. Rhone," I said quietly. "I've got work to do."

SEVENTEEN

Before Miles got back with my camera, a familiar whistle echoed to me, bouncing off the parking garage's mostly concrete structure. I closed my eyes and pinched the bridge of my nose, staving off the man-sized headache walking toward us.

"I thought you wanted to avoid the cops," I said.

Seth grunted. "We didn't call them."

Which meant somebody else had. Great. Just what I needed.

Peterson strolled into view and didn't look at all surprised to see us gathered around a dead body.

"Some party," he said.

"Why are you here?" I ground out.

"I was out getting a donut. Spotted you running a red light. I thought, where's the fire, so I followed you. And here I am, too, just in time. Who's our friend there?"

I gave in to the inevitable as gracefully as I could and knelt with my former partner beside the body. "Don't know yet. Rhone says she's a supe."

On cue, Seth said, "Witch."

Peterson looked at me. "How's he do that?"

"Smell," I said, and left it at that. I pointed to the young woman's ragged fingernails. "Dirt."

"Clawed her way through it or buried?" Peterson angled his head, covered tonight with a plain, dark brown toboggan. "Dirt on her clothes."

"Buried?" I suggested.

"Buried and dug up, maybe."

Miles walked up then with my camera. I took it and cut the flash on. Now that Peterson was here, it was only a matter of time before other cops arrived, too. I had minutes maybe, and I needed to make the most of them.

Peterson squinted up at Seth from where he squatted. "Anybody moved the body since it was discovered?"

"No. We were waiting for Vanessa."

"Vanessa, huh." Peterson shot me an oblique glance, then stood. "Gotta call it in. We'll get the supernatural unit out here. Used to be her job, you know."

He knew. Everyone here did. I wanted to cut the savage thought off at the root, but it grew beyond my control, much like everything else in my life. I raised the camera and started snapping pictures, hoping I captured something that would help me clear my brother's name.

Cops gave supes a lot of leeway, once their involvement was known. A lot of leeway in pretty much everything except murder.

We didn't know that the young woman had been murdered. She'd been placed back down on the concrete with her arms and legs arranged as if she'd fallen. Fully clothed, so her limbs were hidden along with any suspicious breaks or holes where holes shouldn't be. The clothes were intact anyway.

The cynical cop in me didn't take that as a good sign. Someone had left the body here for a reason, and the way the werewolves were acting, especially the one in wolf form, the body had blood on it.

Captain Winifred Jones arrived not too long after, looking spiffy and sharp in a gray suit, her ebony legs bare under the hem of a matching skirt in spite of the night's chill. Technically, her title was Police Chief, since she ran the Crossville PD. But everyone called her Captain, a rank she'd more than earned. She served as a buffer between individual cops and the mayor and citizens, and she'd gone to bat for us more than once, earning our loyalty over and over again.

With her came two patrolmen, who quickly taped off the scene. A forensics team and the ME were not far behind, which must've been a feat. Clearly, Peterson had called the captain as soon as he'd spotted me, well before arriving here. I couldn't fault him for doing his job, but I wished in this one instance he hadn't done it nearly as well as usual.

After a cursory, hands-off look at the body, the captain settled into an empty parking spot across and down from Nick's truck, not twenty feet away. "Peterson," she snapped. "Mr. Rhone. Over here, if you please."

I stayed where I was, out of the way but with a clear view of the body. I wanted to watch the forensics team, another futile effort to dig out a clue before the police could ferry it away.

"Kinley!" the captain said, and I sighed. Yeah, that had been a long shot anyway.

I jogged over to where she stood with Seth and Peterson. Seth's present pack members had faded into the shadows, there but unseen. I could almost feel their eyes on me. It was all I could do not to fidget.

"What happened?" the captain said as soon as I joined them.

Seth ran down a brief summary of the whens and whats, including calling me and my arrival on scene. Peterson picked up from there, rendering me completely unnecessary. I listened with half an ear, the rest of my attention on the body and the people surrounding it. At one point, someone rolled it partially over. Pictures, evidence bags. The captain told us to stay put and strode over, and when she came back, she did not look happy.

"Tarot card under the body," she said. "The Hanged Man."

Peterson hummed under his breath, but Seth looked at me.

"What does it mean?" he said.

"I don't know," I replied, but my skin had gone cold, colder than could be accounted for solely by the chilly October night. The Hanged Man. A diviner I was not, but even I knew you couldn't take tarot cards literally.

Still. That card in isolation, left under a dead body? It had to be a message, one intended for someone here. No, a message intended for Nick.

Or maybe a message aimed at me.

I wrapped my arms around myself and dropped my head, staring blankly at the motor oil-stained concrete beneath my feet. What if Nick wasn't the one being framed here? What if I was the target?

I shook my head. Neither one of us had any enemies that I knew of. Nick led a solid, upstanding life and was well-respected by one and all.

And my days on the PD were behind me, my collars all behind bars or otherwise accounted for. I couldn't think of a single soul from my time as a cop who'd go to such lengths with one body, let alone serial kidnapping other supernaturals.

Assuming everything was connected.

Maybe that was where I'd gone wrong. Maybe the disappearances weren't connected at all and had nothing to do with each other. Maybe this body, the one placed deliberately behind Nick's truck, was a completely unrelated incident.

I scrubbed my hands over my face and resumed observing the cops on scene, even as frustration and fear waged a war within me for dominance. I needed more information, more time to figure things out, but the longer this went on, the less time it felt like I had.

Seth repositioned himself to stand beside me, close enough for my shoulder to brush his arm, and together, we watched and waited.

EIGHTEEN

Peterson released us when they bagged the body and sent it to the morgue. Seth tried to walk me home. I shrugged him off and stalked off alone. I'd had longer days, but not by much. And I still had work to do.

Kinley's was just closing its doors when I trudged through and said hello to Nick. Mariah sat on the same damn barstool she'd occupied earlier. She cocked an eyebrow at me, and I stifled a childish impulse to shoot her a bird.

Gah. I needed sleep.

But I needed to clear my brother's name more.

I went upstairs, changed into sweats, grabbed a snack, and took it downstairs to my office. First thing, I updated the case file for the errant wife and uploaded the pictures from my camera. This was my bread and butter. While I'd had to leave before getting the goods, a first for me, I still had a duty to my client. And I still needed to eat.

Once done, I went into the tiny storage area behind my office where I kept old files. One wall had been set up as an investigation board. I kept a freestanding whiteboard back there, too, for brainstorming ideas when I hit a dead end.

Now, I stacked banker's boxes out of the way, printed off pictures of the missing young women and Billy, and pinned them to the wall. An official ID hadn't been made yet, but Peterson had let it slip that he thought the body belonged to the prodigy witch who'd gone missing some time back. I still had the information gleaned from the supernatural fora, so I added that to the mix, too.

That's when the real work began.

Through the night, I poured over each individual's information, searching for connections and coming up empty every time. School for the three women, nothing for Billy, who'd been in the military, then in a cage learning to control his wolf. Two werewolves, a witch, a vampire. Three females, one male. One of mixed race, one Latina, one white, one of an unknown ethnicity.

They were all supernatural. As far as I could tell, it was the only thing they had in common.

So far. I still had leads to run down for all four. Everything I'd discovered to date had been easily accessible on the internet.

Now it was time for some real legwork, starting with the mysterious Dr. Greely, guest lecturer. I did a cursory search for Sam Greely, astronomy, and came up with pages of hits for Samantha Greely, a professor at Georgia Tech in the Physics department. My brain went into overdrive as I tracked her down through the school's website and her own, as well as social media. Dr. Greely had literally written the book on the search for extrasolar planets, so it was unsurprising that she'd been tagged as a guest lecturer at various area colleges and universities.

I double checked her schedule, conveniently published on her website and blog, against the institutes attended by the other missing supes, and bingo. She'd been to both in the past year pushing her book. Good documentarian that she was, she even had pictures from the events up on her blog.

I scrolled through those, examining each one, and hit on a photo that rang a distant bell. In it, a fit and outwardly happy Dr. Greely stood in front of a folding table on which rested a couple dozen books, copies of her own apparently. She was bracketed by a man and a woman, both students, if the caption could be believed, and in the background, a man stood behind the table with his head partly turned down and his hands apparently arranging things.

The caption described him as "a colleague," but I recognized him from somewhere. White hair, stylishly tousled. Slender in an athletic way. An air of energy clung to him, and that's when it hit me. This was the unknown supe I'd passed on my way into the community college's student center.

Excitement swept through me. I printed that picture, pinned it to the board, and saved a digital copy to my phone. Then I spent half an hour trying to figure out what kind of colleague he was, with absolutely zero results. Finally, I emailed Dr. Greely and asked her outright. When all else fails, be direct, right?

Around three thirty a.m., I gave in to the fatigue fogging my brain and hauled myself upstairs to bed. Before I went, an impulse I couldn't name pushed me to add Mom's picture to the wall. I was tracking missing supernaturals, after all. She seemed to fit the bill.

I found the grimoire Dimitri had given me lying where I'd left it, on the trunk in my bedroom. I got ready for bed, then climbed into it with the thick, leatherbound book and flipped it open to a random page. An intricate drawing of milkweed accompanied short verses written in a language I didn't understand. Latin, maybe?

I closed the grimoire and set it on my nightstand for later study, then fell into a deep dreamless sleep.

The next morning, I discovered Mariah sitting outside my brother's door again.

I curled my upper lip at her, baring my teeth. "Wouldn't let you spend the night on the couch?"

She just stared at me.

I locked my door and went downstairs, grumpy. Mariah

sure did know how to ruin a gal's fun.

First thing, I drove to Angel's and banged on her door again. It was only 8:37 a.m., but what the hell. Her car hadn't moved an inch since I'd visited the day before. I knew damn good and well she was inside.

This time, she refused to come to the door. I pitched my voice loud enough for her to hear it where she stood at the living room window, peeking at me from behind the tenuous protection of café curtains.

"They found a girl dead last night," I said. "There was a tarot card planted under the body. The Hanged Man. I need your help on this, Angel."

I waited for her to say something or come to the door. Stubborn witch stayed right where she was, silent as a tomb.

I shook my head and jogged down her front steps to my car. There was more than one way to skin a cat. I needed info. And I was desperate enough to shell out money to get it.

Most towns of any size have a seedy area. The strip mall where Angel ran her fortune telling business was one of Crossville's, but not the only one, and certainly not the most dangerous. That would be the Depot, the area around the burned-out husk of the old train depot containing the remnants of grain silos and warehouses destroyed by a raging fire during the early 1930s. The factory's owners had built a new depot closer to the factory, leaving the old depot area to rot. Tenements had been built there during the second Great War, and the area had seen a small resurgence for a time, until the gradual shift of clothing manufacturing overseas during the last half of the twentieth century.

Now, the Depot sheltered druggies, the homeless, and those too beat down to make it outside of what was essentially a slum. It's where the serious conmen originated, ones that made Angel's parlor tricks look like rainbows and sunshine.

Conmen like John Rogers, aka Johnny Magnum, a two-bit bookie with just enough magic to run a sharp con. Johnny liked the cash he earned off the desperate and downtrodden, especially since it kept him in the black with the sharks running out of Atlanta, and he sure did enjoy filching green off the well-to-do suburbanites who were stupid enough to drop money in front of him.

But he loved the emotions behind the cons more, loved the slick desperation and quiet fear, the sharp greed and raw anger when a bet went bad.

Johnny was more than a witch toying with forbidden magic; he was a leech suckling the teat of Crossville's underbelly, nurturing his darker nature with the emotions he siphoned off his victims. I'd tried a dozen times to put him away. Somehow, he'd managed to wiggle his way out of a solid conviction every single time.

So I'd used him as a snitch and waited for the moment when I could take him down for good. That hadn't happened before I left the force, but I still touched base with him once in a while. Not just for the information, and Johnny Magnum was good for information, if the price was right. But because someday, somehow, I wanted to see him get his just desserts.

From Angel's, I turned around and drove back to downtown Crossville, then turned toward Depot, jogging through side streets to try to avoid some of the morning's heavier traffic. It was a little early for the crowd Johnny ran with, but he usually kept a room above Silo, a beer joint a block behind the old train depot. If he wasn't there, I had a few other places to look, but my money was on that room.

When I got to Depot, I parked in front of Silo and made sure my car was locked tight. The bar was closed, its grimy windows empty of light and movement. The streets were deserted here, save for the occasional homeless person sheltering in the entryway of an abandoned shop. The stench of rotting garbage permeated the air. Most of the storefronts were barred or boarded up. Some smartass had spray painted "Abandon Hope" in red on the stained plywood covering the old grocery store across the street.

Truth be told, this kind of decay made me sad. Not guilty or ashamed because I'd done better. Just sad. The people living here had lost hope, if they'd ever had any to begin with. They were victims as much of their own inability to see beyond Depot as anything. As a rookie cop, the need to change that, to fix it, had burned brightly within me. Over time, I'd become disillusioned and jaded, and finally stumbled upon an uncomfortable truth: The only way the people here could be helped was if they *wanted* to be helped.

Most didn't. It didn't matter why. You can't help people who don't want to change.

I checked the street again, searching for danger, then found the narrow, doorless entrance to the apartments above Silo. Two flights of steps later, I stepped into the third floor hallway's threadbare, pockmarked carpet. From some unknown room, a television blared a game show, and the scent of curry and old grease hung in the air. The popcorn ceiling had a brown water stain running down the center and a used needle lay against the baseboard.

A hallway much like this one had helped end my career as a cop. It wasn't something I liked to dwell on. Thinking about it wouldn't change the past any more than anger could. But it was hard not to remember as I walked down this hallway. Hard not to remember the gun pointed at me, the sharp report of my own weapon, the heartbreaking truth of how fragile my partnership with Peterson really was.

But I didn't have to worry about that anymore, did I?

I shook my head and gave the discarded needle a wide berth, then found apartment 309 and banged on the door.

A groggy male voice hollered from within, and a moment later, the door cracked open and Johnny Magnum stuck his shaggy head out. He was a runty fellow, maybe half a head taller than me and as gaunt as a seasoned meth addict. A pair of flannel pajama bottoms sagged low on bony hips and a tiny tattoo of a die winked at me from his right ribcage.

I backed up a pace and grinned my best cop grin at him. "Hey, there Johnny. How's it going?"

"Detective Kinley." Johnny sucked on his surprisingly straight, white teeth and opened the door wide. "Fancy seeing you here. You come by to place a bet? Maybe put some money on the Falcons?"

I guffawed. "I like my money where it is, thanks."

He shrugged. "Ain't my fault the Falcons lose so much."

Probably not, unless he paid some of the players off. I doubted it, though. Johnny was too low on the food chain to affect the outcome of a pro football game.

"I'm looking for some info," I said. "Maybe you've heard something."

His brown eyes took on a gleam. "Well, now. That might cost you."

"Maybe so. Serena Jimenez."

"Never heard of her."

"She's one of Seth Rhone's wolves."

The gleam of avarice shifted subtly to wariness. "I don't fuck with Rhone. Nobody does."

I hummed under my breath. Yeah, probably because of Mariah. Hey, I never denied she was good at her job.

"What about Billy Thomas?" I said. "You heard of him?"

"No." The word was short, terse, and Johnny was rigid in the doorway. "You think I got something to do with this?"

"I'm asking for information. You keep your ear to the ground. You hear things."

"Ain't heard nothing about that."

My gut jangled. Johnny was lying, but why? What had he heard?

I slipped my phone out, pulled up the picture of the unknown supe, and flipped it around where Johnny could get a clear view. "You know this guy?"

Johnny's sallow skin paled and sweat dotted his upper lip. "Naw. Never seen him before in my life."

"You sure about that? Here, take a closer look." I shoved

my phone into his hands, then pulled out my wallet and slipped the corner of a Benji out, right where Johnny could see it. "You sure you don't feel like sharing?"

He handed me my phone back and stared me straight in the eye. "Ain't got nothing to share."

My gut jangled again, and I thought, *liar, liar, pants on fire.*

I grunted as I tucked my phone and the Benji away, tugged out a ten, and handed it to him. "Keep the change, Johnny."

He laughed and some of the tension bled out of his stance. "You got balls, Kinley. I'll give you that."

"You remember me when you run across any fresh FYI."

"Yeah, yeah."

The ten disappeared as I turned on a boot heel and strode away. From behind me, Johnny said, "Always a pleasure, Detective. You remember Johnny Magnum when you wanna get a side hustle going."

"In your dreams, Johnny," I said, and he laughed and shut the door.

Good ol' Johnny. Always good for a laugh.

NINETEEN

Since I was out, I swung by Auntie O's to check on her. Unless Nick had texted her with an update, she didn't know the trouble we were in. I could pretty much rule out that update without checking with Nick first. He tried his damnedest not to upset her.

I, on the other hand, could apparently upset her just by being me.

That reminded me. I should've brought the grimoire along and let her look at it. I sighed as I pulled into her driveway and cut off my car's engine. Yeah, probably not the best idea, but I was running out of good ones.

And I had a feeling Nick was running out of time.

An antsy panic niggled in my gut. I hopped out of my car, leaving the door open, jogged to the front door, and knocked.

"Auntie O?" I yelled. "I need to talk to you!"

I heard a rustling from inside, but that was pretty much it. Oscar, the stray tom Auntie fed but couldn't quite tame, slunk around the side of the house and crouched at the corner, his gray furred ears flat against his head.

Maybe she'd gone out to run errands. Auntie was a product

of the '60s and huge on saving the environment. She walked or biked wherever she could, or took the bus in inclement weather. I jogged around to the storage shed and checked it. There sat her shiny red touring bike with its jaunty, daisy covered basket affixed to the front, chained up under the shed's roof, out of the weather, exactly where it was supposed to be when Auntie wasn't using it.

Which struck me as being completely *wrong* for some unknown reason.

I went back to the front entrance and knocked again, buzzed the doorbell, and waited. Finally, after a few minutes without an answer, I tried the doorknob. I had a key, but half the time, she didn't bother locking the door whether she was here or not. I'd warned her over and over again about Crossville's dangerous element, but she'd just smiled and...

Hunh. I looked at the doorknob, puzzled. It turned freely in my hand, but when I tried to pull the door open, it stuck firmly in place. I placed a hand against the frame and yanked hard. The door gave way under my hand, and as soon as it cracked open, a sharp electrical spark shocked my hand.

I yelped and jerked my hand away from the doorknob. The door slammed shut on its own, the lock engaged, and a sinking suspicion filled me.

Auntie had locked herself inside using magic.

My gut clinched on genuine fear. If that were true, Auntie was in terrible danger. Magic was not a toy. I could hear her telling me and Nick, the memory clear through repetition. "Magic is not to be trifled with," she'd say. "It's not a toy or a quick fix. You mustn't use it unless you intend for something to happen, much as you shouldn't load a gun unless you mean to fire it."

If she'd used the kind of magic needed to shut even family out, something was very, very wrong.

I stepped forward and banged my fist against the door, fear lending strength to each blow. "Open up, Auntie. Come on. Open the door!"

Nothing happened, not that time or the time after that, or

the time after that. No matter what I said or how hard I knocked, the door remained firmly shut, with a silent Auntie on the other side.

What if she couldn't answer?

I sucked in that speculation and let my hand drop. The side was red and a little swollen from banging so hard, the palm numb. Speculation was not a useful pastime. Analysis, on the other hand, could be pretty damn useful, and that started with information. What did I know?

I knew that Auntie had likely barricaded herself inside her house using magic, or had made it appear so.

I knew that Johnny Magnum's survival instincts had kicked into gear when I started questioning him.

I knew that something had spooked Angel Miller so badly, she'd pulled her kids out of school and locked herself into her own home.

I knew that someone, somewhere, was responsible for the disappearances of four young supernaturals, one of whom had shown up dead, and that the culprit was either a chaos witch or a close mimic thereof.

And I knew that my brother was not that culprit, not only because his magic was too weak to pull it off, but because he would never harm another person the way those supes had been hurt.

I yanked out my phone and shot off a worried text to Auntie, asking her to text me back right away, if only to let me know she was ok.

Then I got in my car and drove off, my mind tangled around the knowledge that something was very wrong under the surface of sunny Crossville.

My drive home took me right by the Crossville Police Department, my old stomping grounds. The headquarters used to be in the old jail, on the south side of town, but a few years back, someone on the city council had gotten the bright idea to raise funds via a one percent SPLOST for a new building to be built on vacant city land, across from the former primary school, now a community building and park.

The selling point for the council had been combining all emergency services into one easy to maintain complex, thus saving the city money. The new building was closer to the center of what was laughingly called the Crossville Metropolitan area, encompassing the downtown area as well as the adjacent outlying neighborhoods. The central location supposedly cut down on response times and costs such as gas for vehicles.

It worked, but at a steep price. SPLOST hadn't completely covered the building costs, and taxpayers weren't happy. Plus, during less than happy times, the complex was a bigger target, allowing protestors to down the city's entire emergency infrastructure in one go.

It was a big whatever to me. No one had asked the people working out of the old buildings if we'd wanted a new one. Bloom where you're planted, right? And we had, serving the residents of Crossville from the same buildings that had housed generations of cops, fire fighters, and paramedics.

What had Peterson said about the move? Oh, yeah. Progress ain't always what it's cracked up to be.

The captain was in her office when I hit the front desk. I made nice with my former colleagues as I walked toward it, asking after family, joking with work buddies. The atmosphere here had always been great with a few notable exceptions. Close knit. Friendly. I missed it.

A hot spurt of resentment burst through me and I ruthlessly stuffed it down. No use regretting the past. It couldn't be changed, and dwelling on it only ruined the present.

Captain Jones's door was ajar. I rapped on it with my still-sore knuckles and poked my head inside.

"Got a minute?" I said.

She looked up and smiled faintly. "Of course. Is this about the young woman found in the parking deck last night?"

Right. I'd almost forgotten. "Maybe. I've got a possible

lead."

"Come in then."

I entered and closed the door behind myself, then sat in the lone chair placed in front of her desk. The captain's office was sparsely decorated, with a battered wooden desk taking center stage in front of a single bookcase placed against the far wall. A lone rubber tree grew out of a black plastic pot in one corner and a light jacket hung from a coatrack placed in the opposite corner. No filing cabinets, no clutter, no fuss. Even her desk was cleared off, with a laptop open in front of her and a single file in the plastic outbox in one corner of her desk, beside a pencil holder and plain black stapler.

Spartan simplicity. I'd always liked that about the captain.

"What is it you've found?" Captain Jones said.

I gave her my phone with the unknown supernatural's picture showing as I brought her up to date on my findings. Some of it she already knew, if my recent conversations with Peterson could be believed. Surely someone had already put most of this together.

"This guy, though," I said. "I don't know what kind of supe he is or why he was visiting the community college."

"Why do you suspect him then?"

Good question. Difficult, but good. I was following my gut more than anything, feeling out that age-old cop instinct I'd developed here, under her tutelage.

"Right place, right time?" I said.

"That's not enough." She peered at me from under her lashes, giving me a look that sat somewhere between stern and disappointed. "I need more before I can so much as look into him. You know our agreement with the Council."

Ah, yes. The Council, arbiter of everything supernatural. So secret even most supes didn't know exactly who was on it and what they did. Unless you crossed a line. Supes who did were never heard from again, so it's not like they could tell anyone.

"Yeah, I know." I sat back in the chair, settling in with an old familiarity as I struggled to pull my suspicions together. The masculine hand in the one illumination. The strength of Billy being pulled away from the fire in another. The coincidence of Dr. Greely's mysterious colleague being at a lecture Serena had attended, and the strong possibility that he'd had contact in the same way with two of the other young women.

I rolled my shoulders, not sure where to begin, what to tell her. Finally, I settled on, "If he was at those lectures and book signings—"

"Big if."

I waved that one away, even though it was true. "If he was, then it's possible he had access to three of the missing supes. Two," I corrected, "a vampire and a local werewolf, plus the dead witch."

"Detective Peterson tells me there's another werewolf missing," the captain said. "Have you been able to connect him to this unknown supernatural?"

"No," I reluctantly admitted. "Honestly? I haven't definitively tied him to anyone except maybe Serena Jimenez."

"You don't have enough," she said quietly. "Not nearly enough, Kinley, and until you do..."

"I know." I blew a breath out and slumped in the chair. Damn it. Trust the captain to poke holes in my one good hypothesis. "I'll work on it."

"Get Detective Peterson to help you." She raised a hand, forestalling my automatic protest. "I understand that Mr. Rhone has hired you to look into his missing pack members. Peterson can help. He's working one angle, you're working another. It only makes sense to pool resources, especially with the situation escalating like it is."

"Has something else happened?"

"Isn't a dead witch enough?" She smiled faintly again and folded her hands together on top of her desk, in front of the laptop. "Bring me something firm, Kinley. Then we can talk again. And send me a copy of that picture."

"Yes, ma'am." I stood and walked toward the door, then turned halfway back. "I know Seth Rhone is pushing you toward

Nick as the culprit."

Captain Jones gazed steadily at me for a moment. Finally, she said. "I cannot comment on that aspect of the investigation."

My mouth firmed into a hard line, holding in my frustration and a spurt of helpless anger. "Thanks for seeing me."

"Of course. You're always welcome here."

I nodded and turned to the door. Just as I started to open it, she added, "We miss you around here, Vanessa. If you'd stayed—"

"I couldn't stay," I said.

"I understand."

Yeah, she did, mostly because I'd detailed my reasons for leaving in my resignation letter.

I nodded again and left, feeling about as hopeless now as I had when Seth had sicced Mariah on Nick.

TWENTY

My options were narrowing by the moment. Sure, I had avenues I could explore, but not quick ones. Not easy ones. The walls were closing in, faster and faster. I could almost feel the investigation slipping away from me.

I was tempted to dive straight into searching for the unknown colleague of Dr. Greely's. She hadn't emailed me back yet, unless somehow my phone had stopped pinging notifications at me. Until she did, I had a feeling trying to track that guy down was not my best avenue of attack.

What that avenue was, I didn't know. Desperation was beginning to wear a hole in my stomach and worry clouded my mind. I was too close to this. I knew it, the captain knew it. Hell, probably everyone in Crossville knew it, too. I was too close. Too much was at stake. The mere thought of what Seth's wolves would do to Nick if I couldn't figure out who'd really kidnapped Serena and Billy...

My hands tightened into fists at my sides. No. I couldn't think like that. Couldn't think about that at all.

I could, however, check on my brother before I threw myself into the investigation again. Twenty minutes later, I'd parked outside Kinley's and stepped into the bar. What day was it even? I'd lost track.

I scanned Kinley's lunch crowd, looking for Nick. When I couldn't find his handsome face, my heart thumped hard. Where was he? Had something happened to him? He was supposed to be working.

No, wait. I checked my phone, and some of the sick panic receded. It was Tuesday, an off day, if he could manage it. I threaded through the tables, uttering a terse hello when I had to, and checked the office. Empty.

Upstairs, then, taking the steps two at a time. The hallway between our apartments was empty, too, the air dry and stale.

I banged on his front door. "Nick? Open up."

Nothing. Not a sound from inside, not a rattle of the lock being opened. Not anything.

I inhaled a slow breath, yanked my phone out with trembling fingers, and dialed him. Paced down the hallway as the phone rang once, twice.

He picked up in the middle of the third ring. "Hello?"

I slumped against the hallway wall and exhaled shakily. "Where are you?"

"Grocery store. Why? Need me to pick up something?"

"No. Just checking on you."

"Ok." He dragged the word out a fraction of a second too long. "Everything ok?"

I let out a half-hysterical laugh. "Is Mariah still dogging your heels?"

He snickered. "I'm going to tell her you said that. But no. Jamal took over so she could get some sleep."

Oh, even better. "Be careful."

"Sure."

His answer was too breezy by far, but I couldn't find it in me to chastise him for his lack of concern. I had plenty enough for the both of us.

We said our goodbyes, then I slipped into my apartment. A long jog on the treadmill might clear my head, and if that didn't work, I'd start digging again.

* * *

Nothing came to me other than what I already knew needed doing: Tracking down the possible connections between Dr. Greely's colleague and the missing supernaturals.

What bothered me the most about him was that I hadn't been able to identify his race. Witch, werewolf, vampire, elf. He hadn't felt like any of those or a half dozen other types of supernaturals I'd run across over the years. After a while, you got a feel for it. The twitch of an ear here, a glimpse of a fang there, the odor of dried herbs clinging to clothing, all subtle clues that the individual in question wasn't human.

But with this guy? I hadn't a clue. That lack of classification worried at me.

So, too, did the familiar feeling I'd gotten when I'd spotted his picture. I'd seen him somewhere other than the community college, somewhere local, and recently, too. My brain refused to yield an answer, leaving me with not much to go on.

To distract myself, and because I still had bills to pay, I spent the rest of the afternoon and evening tying up regular cases, checking messages, scheduling appointments, and generally catching up on business things. The client who'd asked me to follow his wife checked in with the news that Mrs. CFO had gone out of town again. I hadn't told him about following her to the hotel yet. One night in a hotel did not adultery make. I asked him to text me the moment she came home.

The hours wore on. Nick texted that he'd made it back to his apartment. I locked up my office and followed up on an insurance fraud case, then came back, finished my report, and sent it to the client along with an invoice. A potential client knocked on the door, a lawyer who'd seen my door on his way to Kinley's. She asked about tracking down beneficiaries of an estate. Regrettably, I had to give her the name of another firm specializing in exactly that, as that was not my forte.

Around ten, I decided to call it a day. My desk was clean,

most of my active cases tied up or at a good stopping point. Tomorrow, I'd start chasing down the unknown supe, even if I had to hunt Dr. Greely down in person.

I locked up and walked slowly up the inner staircase to my apartment, stripped down and got ready for bed, then picked up the grimoire and opened it to a random page. Runes, sketches of plants and small animals, spells in a different foreign language than the one I'd spotted before. I flipped through, wishing I knew more about the unknown witch or witches who'd filled the pages, wishing I could understand what he or she had written, and why.

Answers eluded me, and finally, I closed the grimoire and set it on my nightstand as I slipped into bed.

Dimitri knew whose it was. No doubt about that. But I was not calling a vampire into my apartment at night for a second time, or ever, if I could help it at all.

Something trilled, waking me from a dead sleep. I sat bolt upright, my hand reaching automatically for the gun holstered beside my bed.

The trilling came again, and I realized that someone was calling me at...

I squinted at my alarm clock and huffed out a tired breath. Five thirty-seven a.m. Lovely. At least I'd gotten more than two hours' sleep this time.

I flipped on the bedside light and checked my phone.

And was somehow unsurprised to see Peterson's name and number scrawled across the screen.

I opened the line and said, "This had better be good."

"Good isn't the word I'd use," he said. "Where were you last night around nine?"

I shoved a hand through my hair, pushing it away from my face, and yawned as I calculated where I'd been. "In the office probably. Why?"

"I'm looking at the body of John Timothy Rogers."

My heart stopped beating for a full two seconds, then

thumped into overdrive, hammering against my sternum. "Shit."

"You remember John, don't you? Went by Johnny Magnum?"

"Cut the crap, Peterson. Where'd you find him?"

"You don't know?"

"How could I? I'm in bed where I was sleeping soundly until you called me."

"You sure you wanna see this one, Kinley?"

I stifled a low curse. Damn misogyny of his was kicking in again. "Just give me the address."

"Down at the station."

I waited for the punchline, and when it didn't come, said, "Stop kidding around, Peterson."

"I wish I were."

His voice had gone soft and quiet, and that scared me more than anything.

I swallowed hard and slid out of bed. "I'm on my way."

"I got questions."

I just bet he did. Probably not as many as I had, though. "Be there in thirty."

I hung up without saying goodbye or, better, cussing him out, which was more than Peterson deserved by far.

TWENTY-ONE

It took me twenty minutes to get to the station and another five to push my way through the people crowded onto the sidewalk. Though the eastern horizon had lightened, heralding the coming day, it was still dark out, dark enough that the flashing blue and red lights of emergency vehicles cast an odd, disco-like effect over the scene.

My phone buzzed, just loud enough for me to hear. I pulled it out and saw a text from Auntie O.

Oh, thank God.

I thumbed into it and read, *The cards don't lie, but they're not always right.*

Well, wasn't that as helpful as mud on a windshield.

I hit the dial button and waited for her phone to ring. Instead, I got a prerecorded voice saying, "The number you dialed has been disconnected."

Shit.

Ok, crime scene first, and then I was by golly going to track Auntie down to see what the hell was going on with her.

A patrol cop saw me and waved me over, and when I reached her, I sucked in a breath. Johnny Magnum was hanging upside down from the flagpole with one leg straight and the other bent at the knee so that the ankle rested on the other knee. Blood dripped down his body from various lacerations, obscuring his face, but there was no mistaking who it was, or what he represented.

The Hanged Man.

"Makes you wonder how the hell they got him to stay like that, don't it?" Peterson said from my left.

I glanced at him and away from the bloody mess that had been a man just a few hours ago. "Since you've been at the scene a while, I'm sure you already know."

"Yup, we do. Question is, do you?"

"I don't know squat about it."

"Izzat so?" Peterson waved a hand at Johnny's body. "Your snitch."

"Yes, he was."

"You see him recently?"

I had and wasn't that a huge coincidence.

"Sure," I said. "I'm a regular down at his illegal gambling den. Just can't stay away from the card table. Oh, and while I was there, I put a Benji down on Sunday's game, just for shits and giggles."

Peterson stared at me for a minute. I could almost see the wheels turning in that squirrelly little brain of his.

"Ayup," he finally said. "We know you were one of the last people to see him alive. His neighbors got real talkative when they learned about the dearly departed."

"Am I a suspect?"

"Should you be?"

"If you think that, you never knew me."

Peterson's gaze sharpened, then he shook his head and turned that look on Johnny, hanging from the flagpole in an irreverent imitation of Christ on the cross.

Judging me. Always judging, and damned if I wasn't tired of coming up short in my old partner's eyes.

"Screw you, Peterson," I said, my voice low and strangled

with the old anger and bitterness.

"Sure, Kinley. Name the date and place and I'll be there."

I croaked out a strangled laugh. "Are you out of your mind?"

"Not that I recall." He pointed to Johnny again. "Cap'n says you got somebody in mind for this."

For a moment, betrayal overlaid the familiar bitterness, but I pushed it aside. Of course, Captain Jones had shown Peterson the picture I'd given her. There was a murderer on the loose, and he was her best homicide detective, not to mention the only one with any real knowledge of the supernatural world.

I rolled my shoulders, forcing them to relax, and let my gaze follow Peterson's to the crime scene. "Maybe, but I can't tie him to any of this. Not definitively."

"Not your brother then."

"The hell?" I said.

Peterson shrugged. "We already have a file on him. For my money, he's not good for this."

My laugh held all the bitterness I'd tried to push away. "Do you believe that, or are you just saying it for my benefit?"

"Maybe you never knew me so well either, Kinley," he said, so low I almost missed it under the uneasy murmurs of the people gathered around the crime scene despite the late hour.

I barked out a hard laugh. "I knew you too well."

With a sigh, I stepped toward the scene, intending to get a closeup look. Peterson's hand shot out and grabbed me, holding me in place. I looked at him, just looked, and he let go.

"We found another tarot card," he said. "The Empress."

My skin went cold. The Empress, the very card Angel Miller had pulled over and over again the last time she'd read the cards for me, when I'd been hunting the person responsible for burning down part of Seth's development. A mother, she said, and I'd thought *no*, a mother figure.

Auntie O.

My heart trembled in my chest. I placed a hand over it as I opened my phone and called her again. The same mechanical voice answered, informing me that the number had been disconnected, and I cursed under my breath.

"What?" Peterson said.

"Nothing."

"Kinley."

I ignored his warning tone. "When can I access the reports for the two deaths?"

He didn't bother asking which two I meant. "I'll see what I can do."

"You do that."

My phone beeped again, and for one brief second, hope surged. Auntie O was getting back to me. But when I flipped it over and looked, it was a text from my brother. I opened it, and what I read nearly made me stagger.

Seth took me into custody on behalf of the Council.

No. That couldn't be right!

I texted Nick, letting him know that I was on the way.

"You should really talk to me," Peterson said.

"Can't," I replied. "Gotta go. Keep me in the loop."

He nodded, though he still hadn't looked at me again. "Seems like somebody's gunning for you, Kinley. Planting a body next to your brother's truck, now another one across from the police station where you used to work. You didn't by any chance go to school here, when it was a primary school?"

Yes. Yes, I had, me and Nick both, and that wasn't the only evidence that someone might be targeting us. But why? Why would anyone go to such lengths to frame us? Or were they merely trying to get our attention?

The questions started an endless, worrisome loop in my head, and I was fresh out of answers.

"I gotta go," I said again, then I thanked him for calling me and went to try to save my brother.

I went straight to Seth's house and parked behind Mariah's Bronco. The sun had popped over the horizon as I was driving, lending a thin October light to the morning's mist. Still, every light in his house seemed to be on and then some. Must be some party, I thought on a new surge of bitterness.

The front yard and porch were empty. I walked up the rockwork stairs and through the entrance without knocking, which is what Seth got for leaving his front door unlocked. Inside, I'd expected to find people. Seth's sister or members of the pack. Seth or his lieutenants, at least.

The front part of the house seemed to be empty, though. I couldn't even make out the sounds of a rising household. If someone was here, they were being quiet, or they were in a part of the house distant enough from the front door for sound not to carry well.

I shut the door and walked quickly through the house toward the kitchen, leaving the front door unlocked. Trudy was standing at the island with her hands flat against the mottled granite countertop. She looked up when I entered and her mouth twisted into a weird little smile.

"Come to see wolf justice?" she said.

The question shocked me into a standstill. "Already?"

She shook her head and pushed away from the island, turning away from me toward the too-clean stove. "Seth took Nick upstairs to a secure bedroom."

My legs went weak with relief. I staggered to the table and sat heavily in a chair before they gave out entirely and dumped me on the floor. "Nick has solid alibis. There was a murder tonight."

Trudy whipped back around, her eyes wide. "Who?"

"An old snitch of mine." I held up a hand, forestalling questions before she could ask them. "I don't know who did it. I don't know why. The police are handling it."

She closed her mouth and nodded slowly, then twisted her long hair into a knot on top of her head. "I'd better get some breakfast started."

I almost offered to help. Automatic politeness. Mom had done that much right at least. "I'll wait for Seth in the den."

She nodded again and reached for the refrigerator's handle, her mind clearly already on preparing the coming meal. I stood and jiggled the weakness out of my legs.

As I turned to go, Trudy said, "Don't antagonize him, Nessa. He's already close to the edge."

I didn't need two guesses to know she was talking about Seth. With a heavy sigh, I backtracked through the house to the den and sat down on one of the comfy couches.

Seth came down half an hour later, trailed by Jamal, his silent and overly large training lieutenant.

I'd been fidgeting on the couch, fighting yawns. As soon as I heard their footsteps, I leapt up and faced the door separating the foyer from the den, waiting for them to see me.

"Why?" I said. "You know he didn't do this."

Seth raked a hand through his hair, tousling it as Jamal walked silently around us and stood at the opposite end of the massive couch, facing us. They both looked tired, not quite haggard. That was fine with me. The last few days had exhausted me, too. Still, I had work to do.

"It wasn't entirely up to me," Seth said.

I laughed. "Yeah, it was."

One corner of his mouth turned down into half frown. He hooked his hands on his hips over the hem of his long-sleeved t-shirt. "You're being irrational."

"I'm not the one who's being irrational here!"

"And you're yelling. My wolf doesn't like it when you yell."

"Then listen to me," I said flatly.

His eyes, normally a murky green-brown hazel, took on an amber cast. "I listen to you. All the damn time, I listen. Have you heard anything I've said?"

"What have you said? That you have to take him in? That it wasn't your choice?" I threw my hands up in the air, so tired of being helpless I could've hit something. "Looks to me like this was entirely your choice, Seth. *You* were the one who assigned

Mariah to him. *You* were the one who caged him within your own house. *You*, Seth. No one else."

"Nessie," he began, and I cut him off with a furious slash of my hand.

"I told you not to call me that."

Between one breath and the next, he'd wrapped his hands around my upper arms and lifted me so that my face was so close to his, I could see the black flecks hiding in the amber of his irises. I froze in his grasp, too afraid to move, too terrified. His wolf was out. I hadn't said anything to push him, I thought frantically. We'd had harsher words than that more than once. Not often, but enough. If I hadn't provoked him then, why was this discussion provoking him now?

Trudy had said he was close to the edge. I hadn't realized she meant he was already there.

A low, growly rumble emanated from Seth's throat. "I will call you anything I want to, Nessie. Any. Damn. Thing."

"Seth," Jamal said quietly.

"*Mine*," Seth growled.

Shock cut through the terror. I was not Seth's. Not once had he ever hinted that I might be a potential mate or anything other than casual friends. We'd never even hugged, that I could recall. Or was he talking about something else entirely? Werewolves could be territorial, and I, as his renter and the sister of a friend, was loosely part of Seth's territory. It seemed like a stretch, but was that what he'd meant?

I wasn't about to ask, not while he teetered on the edge of change. If Seth lost control...

I swallowed and shoved that thought out of my head. No. Couldn't think about that now.

I lowered my eyes and rolled my head to the side, exposing my throat, submitting as much as I could. It was the only thing I could think of to appease his wolf. He was the dominant here. I was the wee half witch, weak and helpless as a mewling kitten before him.

Slowly, his breathing calmed and the amber faded from his

eyes. Just as slowly, he lowered me. When my feet touched the floor, he released his grip on me, and I kept on going, sinking into the couch behind me.

A dull, throbbing pain flooded into my upper arms. I bit my lip to hold in a whimper and curled toward my knees, protecting my softer flesh in case his wolf was still ascendant and he attacked. Not that it would do any good. Seth made two of me, most of it muscle and bone. I didn't stand a chance against him.

He knelt beside me and tentatively touched my shoulder. It was all I could do not to jerk away. He must've felt me twitch, though, because he sighed and dropped his hand.

"Did it never occur to you that other supernaturals are calling for Nicky's death?" he said. "That he really is safer here under my protection, where no one would dare try to take him until we can find who really did this?"

I couldn't answer. My tongue seemed frozen to the roof of my mouth and my courage had fled the minute he'd grabbed me.

He rolled into a stand. "Ok. Stay here until you're calm enough to drive. Use one of the bedrooms, if you want. Trudy or Jamal can show you where my bedroom is, if you'll feel safer there when the rest of the pack gets here."

A breathy laugh worked its way out of my throat. Stay in Seth's bedroom? I doubted I'd ever feel safe standing in the same room as him, let alone entering his bedroom.

His legs moved out of my line of sight, and I heard him and Jamal leave the room. That was when I realized that I was doing more than trembling. I lifted a shaky hand to my face and discovered wet cheeks, and I did laugh then, hysterical sobs that made me question whether I was laughing or crying.

TWENTY-TWO

When I'd calmed down, I cleaned up in the half-bath off the foyer, then went upstairs and talked the twenty-something male standing outside my brother's bedroom prison into letting me check on Nick. The young werewolf compromised by opening the door and letting me chat with my brother so long as I kept my back to the opposite wall and Nick didn't leave the bedroom.

I was desperate enough to take what I could get.

Nick was wearing an old concert t-shirt over red and gray plaid pajama bottoms. His hair was mussed and his feet were bare, and just looking at him, knowing he was ok, made me relax into the wall in relief.

"Hey," I said. "You look tired."

"Normally asleep right not." His mouth curled into a sleepy, familiar half smirk. "You look like crap."

"There you go, winning that brother of the year award again."

He laughed. "Yeah, that's me. Brother of the year."

"You shouldn't have let her in."

"Nessie."

I ignored the quiet patience in his voice. "I know you're innocent. You've got alibis for most of the disappearances and two murders."

"Seth said that's why they brought me here. A second murder."

So he'd known about it before me. Nice heads up there, Rhone.

"Peterson's working it," I said.

Nick cursed low and long under his breath.

I managed a weak smile. "He's really working it, Nick. I've given them some of what I've found. They have resources I don't."

I couldn't say that I'd hit a wall I might not be able to tear down with him being held in the lion's den. Having that in his head wouldn't do Nick any good at all.

Instead, I said, "I'm still working some angles."

It was a lie, but not too much of one. I hoped it wasn't too much of one anyway.

Nick exhaled sharply and looked down at where his bare toes curled into the neutral tan carpet. Always so at home here, always so at ease.

I sighed and pushed away from the wall, rousing the young man from his position beside Nick's door.

"I'll be back to check on you," I said. "Need anything?"

"Naw. Seth's making sure I'm taken care of."

Yeah, sure, I thought, but I bit my tongue.

We said goodbye, leaving our usual love yous unspoken, and I went back out to my car to try to find answers while I still had time.

As soon as I was on the road, I called Auntie one last time, and got the disconnected message again.

Swearing, I pointed the car toward her house while I dialed Angel. The call went straight to voice mail. Not what I'd hoped for, but a decided improvement over not talking to her at all. I left a message detailing as much as I could safely share about the tarot cards and asked her to call me.

By then, I was almost to Auntie's house. I parked in her driveway and pulled out my to key to her front door, which I should've done yesterday. Would've if my head were on straight.

My phone beeped. I opened it and found a text from Auntie.

Why is Benjamin Franklin in my latest reading?

I glanced automatically at the keys in my hand. Metal keys. Electric shock spell.

I dropped my forehead to the steering wheel. Damn it. But a text had gotten through, so surely that meant I could get one back to her. I dropped my keys and shot back a quick *you ok?*

And got a delivery failure notice.

How the hell was she getting texts through to me?

Frustrated, I stomped up the path to her front door and hammered on it, yelling at her loud enough for the neighbor across the street to hobble out. Mr. Monteith, a grizzled, ninety-three-year-old chemistry teacher who'd put the fear of God into three generations of Crossville youth. Bless him, he'd thrown a flannel robe over his cotton pajama set and wore shoe-like slippers, hopefully with enough tread to keep him from slipping on the lightly frosted grass.

"Have some respect, Vanessa Kinley," he hollered. "Your caterwauling could wake the dead, and it barely past the cock's crow."

I walked to the edge of Auntie's yard and, duly chastened, lowered my voice. "Hello, Mr. Monteith. Have you seen Auntie Ophelia in the past few days?"

"Seen her? Of course, I have," he replied. "We had tea two days ago, just like we always do."

"What about yesterday?"

"What about it? We don't have tea on Mondays, young lady, which you know very well."

Oh, I knew that all too well, from the decade plus of having Auntie as a surrogate mom. "Have you seen anyone strange hanging around her house?"

"Only you, Vanessa, and that's quite enough, don't you think?"

He bent down and picked up the rolled copy of the newspaper someone had dropped behind his mailbox, then turned around and went inside as if I weren't still standing there with questions needing answers.

I sighed and ran my hands over my hair, trying to reason through this dilemma. Auntie O's magic was likely strong enough to protect her. I didn't feel right leaving her house again without seeing that she was definitely, one hundred percent okay, not after The Empress tarot card turned up near Johnny Magnum's body.

On the other hand, I couldn't stand out here all day, trying to find a way to talk to her. If she didn't want to see me, there was nothing I could do. That's all there was to it.

Auntie O could take care of herself.

The wrongness of that thought curled sickly inside my stomach, but I didn't know what else to do.

With another sigh, I dug around in my car for pen and paper, scrawled out a quick note, and stuck it under the doormat, where she could retrieve it without risking her safety overly much.

I slid inside my car, shut the door, and pulled out my phone. A minute later, I dialed Dr. Greely's office phone number, found during a quick search of Georgia Tech's website, and stared at Auntie's front door while it rang.

A moment later, Greely's voice mail kicked in. Damn it all to hell, but I could not catch a break, and I desperately needed one.

I left a terse message reminding her of the email I'd sent, then rattled off my contact info and hung up. The front door hadn't budged an inch during the call. I dropped my phone in the passenger's seat and gripped the steering wheel with both hands until the knuckles whitened and my fingers hurt.

I had one more ace up my sleeve, one more contact I could

call on before I had to start digging again. Unfortunately, it was one that was going to break my three nevers into a million tiny pieces.

TWENTY-THREE

When I got back to the office, I headed straight to the storage room, pulled out a chair, and sat down facing my case board, staring at Mom's picture while I worked up the nerve to call Dimitri. A phone would've been better, but no, he'd had to go initiate some weird blood bond thing.

I didn't even know what to call it.

The thought pushed a weak laugh out of me. I bent at the waist, planted my elbows on my knees, and rested my head in my hands. How did I do this again? Something about rubbing the scar and thinking hard, maybe focusing on Dimitri coming here. Or something.

I shifted so that one thumb rested over the tiny, pink scar. It hadn't quite healed yet, though it had scabbed over and stopped tingling, so maybe it wouldn't work. Maybe it had healed too much.

I tried anyway, pressing my thumb against the mark he'd given me while repeating his name in my mind. For good measure, I said, "Dimitri, you cold-hearted, bloodsucking vamp. I need help. You wanted me to call, and now I am, so—"

I clamped my mouth down around the last word, hoping to staunch the panic trying to gush out. He had to come. He had to help. Hadn't he said he would?

Yeah, but when had anyone ever been able to count on a vampire?

I let go of my wrist and sat back, my gaze drawn unerringly to Mòm's picture. What did I really know about her disappearance? Not the one Dimitri had contacted me about, but the time she'd disappeared on me and Nick. What did I really know about *her*? I sifted through memories, searching for a jumping off point for learning more.

It took time. The memories were buried deep, faded from the intervening years. God knew, I'd done everything I could to forget about her, to forget the good along with the bad. It all hurt equally, every bright smile, every hard word, making the memories all the more difficult to revive.

Finally, though, they started bubbling to the surface, slowly at first, then more quickly, each memory leading to another.

I retrieved a pen and a fresh notebook, and jotted down pertinent moments, whatever seemed helpful. Who knew her? What did she like doing? What places had she returned to? Neighbors, friends, stores she'd visited, hobbies, anything.

When those tapered off, I flipped forward a few pages and wrote down everything I knew about chaos witches and how they practiced magic. Names, rituals, resources, whatever I could think of.

Something in there had to be useful.

My hand started cramping long before I was finished. I stopped and stretched my fingers out when the pain became too difficult to work around, then stood and stretched the rest of me. I'd been sitting for...

I checked the time on my phone and winced. A couple of hours. No wonder my muscles were stiff.

I needed thinking time now, but first, Dr. Greely. She still hadn't contacted me. Instead of bugging her again, I looked up the Physics department chair, a Dr. Jeremy Owens, and called him. Thankfully, he answered on the first ring. I explained who I was and what I was looking for to the gruff voice on the other end.

After a slight pose, Dr. Owens said, "Dr. Greely took an unexpected leave of absence last week."

"Oh," I said, nonplussed. Well, that put a crimp in things. "Did she say why?"

"No, she didn't."

His tone of voice implied that he wouldn't tell me even if she had. I admired his loyalty, but it wasn't exactly helpful to me right now.

"Do you have an idea of when she'll be back?"

"No, Miss Kinley, I do not. I'll be happy to take your contact information and leave it in her inbox, if you'd like."

With a small sigh, I rattled off the best ways to contact me, thanked Dr. Owens for his time, and hung up. My brain was full, my hope nonexistent, and my stomach decidedly grumpy from a lack of food. I locked the office and went upstairs using the inner staircase. Food and a long run would clear my head, then I could dive back into freeing Nick until sunset and the hoped for arrival of Dimitri Stanislov.

Seth was sitting on my couch when I unlocked my apartment door.

My stomach shrank into a queasy knot in my gut, and I fought down the frightened, hurt little girl inside me. Fear would not help, especially around a creature that could literally smell it on me.

I mustered my courage and shut the door, then leaned back against it, hopefully hiding the shakiness of my knees behind the casual pose.

"What do you want, Seth?" I said.

He glanced at me, his rocky features taciturn. "Any progress?"

"On what? Finding the missing wolves? Clearing my brother's name?" That last came out sharper than I'd intended. I forced my shoulders down, reached for some calm. "Why are you here, specifically?"

"Wanted to check on you. Make sure you're ok."

I snorted out a tired laugh. "Right."

"I do." His voice had softened. "You set me off—"

"That's no excuse for grabbing me."

His lips compressed into a thin line. My shoulders hunched again as I tensed, ready to whirl around and flee, but his eyes stayed exactly the same warm color they usually were.

"I'm trying to protect you, Nessie."

I did laugh then. "Yeah, protect me. That's what you've been doing."

"I am. We just need definitive proof."

"Alibis, Seth. How many ways do I have to remind you before you hear me?"

The apples of his cheeks went pink, though he held my gaze. "If it were up to me, things would be different."

I had a feeling he was talking about more than this situation, but I let that go. Sufficient unto each day are the troubles thereof. "He's all I have, Seth. Everything."

"You have me."

The unexpectedness of his response sucked the breath out of me. What did that even mean?

It took about half a second for me to decide that I didn't want to know, didn't *care* to know.

"You're tied to the pack, Seth," I gritted out, "and too many wolves want Nicky dead. Isn't that right, Seth? Doesn't your pack want revenge for the kidnappings? Don't they want you to meet force with force and eliminate any and all threats to the pack?"

He started to speak, and I cut him off with an angry slash of my hand. I didn't need to hear him say it. Anyone who'd had even a small amount of contact with a werewolf pack knew what they were like: Full of aggressive pride, bristling to defend their brother and sister wolves, their families.

"How long can you control their bloodlust?" I continued. "How long can you hold off the Council or whoever it is that seems to be pulling your strings?"

He stood abruptly, his hands in loose fists at his side, and I forced myself not to flinch, to hold my ground. I couldn't be afraid of him forever. Wouldn't. If he was going to hurt me again, let him do it now and get it over with.

But he didn't leap for me. Didn't move a muscle, as a matter of fact. He just stood there glowering.

"Don't ever question my dominance again, Nessie." His voice was more growl than human, almost gravelly in its intensity. "It's one thing to challenge me. Questioning my authority and control over my wolves crosses a line you can't uncross. As for the Council, their say in how I run my pack is nonexistent. That's my territory, my wolves, my people."

"Is Nick your people, too?" The question popped out of my mouth without warning. I wouldn't call it back even if I could. "He looks up to you, you know. His friend, the alpha of the local pack. Protector. Isn't that what you're supposed to be doing here?"

"I am," he said again, but I shook my head and turned away from him.

"You need to leave now, Seth. I have things to do, places to be."

I didn't hear his footsteps on the carpeting so much as feel him approaching me. The skin on my spine crawled, warning me of a predator at my back, but I couldn't move, couldn't face him again.

"What places?" he said.

"Atlanta. A professor at Tech may have a lead on a possible suspect."

He hummed under his breath, then moved around to face me and tilted my chin up gently, forcing me to meet his gaze. "I can't let you go."

"Let me…"

"Go? You can't. The Council wants you here, where we can keep an eye on you."

The implications struck me immediately and my eyes went wide and disbelieving. "I'm a suspect?"

"Not exactly."

"Then what?"

He dropped his hand and stepped back, his gaze suddenly cool and remote. "Stay where I can find you."

"Or what?"

"You don't want to know the answer to that question, Nessie."

I swallowed down the urge to remind him yet again that he didn't have permission to call me that. The last time I'd called him out for the overfamiliarity, he'd manhandled me. I wasn't eager to repeat that experience anytime soon.

And I was tired, so tired. If I couldn't track down Dr. Greely, what hope did I have of following up on the most promising lead I'd found? So what if instinct was the only thing driving my search for him? My instinct had always been on the mark where my job was concerned. It wouldn't fail me now.

But if I knew Seth at all, the moment I stepped foot beyond Crossville's city limits, a wolf would drag me back. Then I'd end up in a cushy cage next to my brother, and what good would that do him?

I ran a hand over my face. Ok, then. I'd just find a way around the obstacle like I always did. Couldn't do that with a two-hundred- and twenty-five-pound werewolf taking up a good chunk of real estate in my living room.

"Go away," I said quietly.

"Nessie..."

"Just go."

I walked around him and went into the kitchen, and stood with my back to the door until I heard it shut softly behind him.

TWENTY-FOUR

Dimitri didn't come after sunset, or after midnight, or before the sun rose and tinted the eastern sky a watery pink.

I'd spent the time hammering away at Dr. Greely's colleagues, emailing them pictures of the unknown supe in the hopes that one of them knew who he was. When I ran out of professors and teaching assistants to harass, I switched to tracking down Mom's old friends and haunts, what I could remember of them.

Auntie O would've been my best source, but she'd remained stubbornly silent.

Why? What had spooked her so much that, like Angel Miller, she'd gone to ground, hiding in her house like a rabbit cowering in the grass from the gaze of a circling hawk?

Finally, after spending the entire night twitching every time the wind blew, I stumbled into my bedroom and fell across the bed, asleep as soon as my head hit the mattress.

When I dragged myself out of bed a few hours later, I discovered Jamal sitting outside my apartment, his back against Nick's front door, his long legs stretched out in front of him.

For a brief moment, hope filled my heart. Nick was back!

Then reality crashed down around me, and I realized that Jamal was there to make sure I didn't flee town.

Great. A guard. Just what I needed.

I went back into my apartment and tucked my Glock into the small of my back. If I was going to be shadowed by a werewolf all day, then I would by golly have some stopping power at my beck and call.

"I'm not feeding you," I said as I reentered the hallway.

He grunted, which I took to mean that he'd already eaten. Probably a helpless little bunny, maybe even Bambi.

I squinted at him, trying to picture his wolf. Yeah, he was definitely a Bambi killer.

I shut my apartment door and locked it. "Gotta get to work now."

He grunted again and pushed himself into a stand. I shook my head and let him trail me. Gah. How the hell was I supposed to track down leads with Jamal ghosting my every step?

On the other hand...

I glanced at him over my shoulder. "I have to go to Atlanta to follow up on a lead."

"No," he said.

Well, that was that then.

With a sigh, I walked downstairs and into my office. Boy, was it going to be a long day.

Around suppertime, Jamal was replaced by a smug Mariah.

"Seth was always too soft on you and Nick," she said in a low, savage growl. "It's time you grew up and learned your place in the hierarchy."

I looked her straight in the eye and said, "Fuck. You."

If she was offended, it didn't show.

But man, was I tired of this crap.

I pointed at the receptionist's office. "Sit in there. Leave me alone."

She crossed her arms over her chest and tried to stare me down with eyes gone bright and wolfy. "Seth said not to let you out of my sight."

I snorted. "Like you can't hear every move I make. Go away, Mariah."

She growled and snapped her teeth at me, and I whipped out my Glock and pointed it at her, aiming for a kill shot, dead center of her chest.

My draw had been nearly as fast as her aggressive bite. I flicked the safety off to get the point across, and because *dayum.* I *really* wanted to shoot her.

"Try it, bitch," I said.

Her lips curled back, baring her teeth, but she backed up and retreated to the receptionist's office. I waited until I heard a chair squeak under her slight weight, then reached for my phone and texted Seth one-handed, my gun still aimed at the doorway.

Send someone else or so help me, I'll shoot Mariah.

There. That ought to rattle his cage.

Slowly, I set my Glock aside, well within easy reach, and turned my attention back to tracking down any lead I could from where I sat.

TWENTY-FIVE

An hour later, I heard rustling noises coming from the outer office. I ignored them, keeping my head down and my gaze focused on the Facebook page displayed there. An old family friend. The face had been nagging me all morning, and I'd finally hit on the surname (Holstein) and location (College Park) and found what I thought might be the family in question.

They were witches. The man was anyway. He'd run a store on the south side of the Metro Atlanta area when we were kids. I distinctly remembered the sharp scent of licorice mingling with the deliciously floral aroma of dried Sweet Annie.

Mr. Holstein had died a few years back. Heart attack. But his wife would remember Mom. Maybe it was time to renew our acquaintance.

Mariah appeared in the doorway, her expression grim. "There's trouble at Seth's. I have to go."

I closed the laptop without clicking out of the browser and casually laid my hand on the Glock's grip. If Mariah noticed, she ignored it. Fine by me. I was still raring to shoot her.

When she didn't continue, I said, "What kind of trouble?"

"I don't know." She cocked her head and her gaze went distant, as if she were listening to something only she could hear. "Bad trouble. Stay here. Lock the doors. Do not leave this building."

"Aye, aye, Captain sir."

The smart-ass remark hid my concern. Trouble at Seth's meant trouble for Nick, and that was not the kind of trouble he needed right now.

Mariah pointed a slender finger at me. "Lock the door behind me."

"Just go already," I said as I stood.

She pivoted and was gone before I'd cleared the desk. I reached the door in time to watch her hop into her Bronco and drive off through the lettering on the outside of the glass door, her taillights a bright red smear against the nighttime street courtesy of a light drizzle.

Vanessa Kinley, Private Investigator.

I shook my head. Yeah, some investigator I was. I hadn't been able to find enough evidence to point to a definitive suspect, let alone convince anyone in the supernatural community that my brother had not committed any crimes. Of course, the supernatural world didn't operate exactly like the human one. There was no presumption of innocence, though it wasn't quite guilty on sight either.

I flipped the door lock and cut the office's lights. No way in hell was I staying put, Mariah's command or not. Nicky might be in trouble. I couldn't abandon him to the pack's dubious protection.

Before I'd taken three steps, the flash of blue lights cut through the darkness. I turned around and watched the front end of Peterson's personal vehicle skid to a stop accompanied by the squeal of rubber against slick asphalt.

Why did I have a funny feeling that his arrival was directly related to Mariah's departure?

I went back to the door and unlocked it, stuck my head out, and yelled, "Where's the fire?"

Peterson glanced at me as he slid out of his car and stood inside the open driver's side door, one foot on the pavement and the other still inside. "Are you armed?"

No. I'd left the Glock on my desk when I'd followed Mariah to the exit. He didn't need to know that.

"Why?" I said.

"I heard Nick's in trouble."

I snorted. "That's old news."

"New trouble. Shit."

My eyebrows shot up as Peterson disentangled himself from his Buick and jogged across the street. One, Peterson did not curse. Ever. And two, he never hurried unless something serious was going on.

That jangling in my gut morphed into jingle bells and stomping reindeer.

I held the door open and let him duck inside. "If you're talking about whatever's going on at Seth's, I already know."

"Do you now." He shook rain from his hair and faced me, looking more like a cop in plain clothes than most cops did in a uniform. "I came to help."

That earned an outright guffaw. "I don't need your help, Peterson. Seriously. Don't need it."

"Yes, you do." He whirled away from me and cursed a blue streak under his breath, then turned right back around and jabbed a finger at me. "Quit being such an independent, stubborn assed mule, Vanessa. I swore to your father—"

That got my attention in a hurry. "What about my father?"

Peterson's jaw worked, grinding his molars together. "I swore I'd keep an eye out for you, and I have."

My temper went from mildly annoyed to spewing hot lava in three milliseconds flat. "Oh, yeah? How about when Truman snuck into the ladies' and tried to grope me? Were you keeping an eye out for me then?"

He had the grace to drop his gaze. "I did what I could."

"Bullshit, Rick. Bullshit! When I told you about it, what did you say?" I snapped my fingers and touched a finger to my temple. "Oh, wait. I remember now. 'Grow up, little girl. You wanna play with the big boys, you gotta get a little dirty sometimes.'"

He deflated like a stuck balloon. "Everybody makes mistakes, Kinley. I learned my lesson when you quit the force."

"I learned mine, too, right after you refused to back me up the next time we went on a call. All because I reported Truman's roaming hands to the captain."

I heaved a sigh and ground the heels of my palms against my closed eyes, trying to rub away some of my anger. Water under the bridge. Nothing anyone could do about it now. Getting angry, and yeah, I was pissed, but that didn't help, even though I wanted to rage at him, to throw something and scream at how much his betrayal had hurt.

I dropped my hands and faced him head on.

"That was the straw, Peterson. Not Truman getting handsy, not the shitshow of having my entire career examined with a fine-toothed comb over having to shoot a suspect. You didn't have my back, and I needed you to." I swallowed the bitterness down and refused to let a single tear fall. Not now. Not in front of him. "I learned my lesson that day, so well I had to quit for fear of being placed in the same situation again. In danger, with my partner, the man I trusted with my life, fading into the background, leaving me to face an armed suspect alone. That's why I quit, Peterson, because you left me and I couldn't trust you anymore."

The silence stretched between us, broken by a car speeding past on the street outside, by the wind sluicing rain against the door. Headlights sliced into the room through the door, illuminating Peterson's face. His eyes were tight at the corners, the lines around his mouth deep grooves. He looked like he'd aged two decades since he walked in.

Me, too, maybe. It wasn't something I wanted to remember, let alone relive, but there Truman was in a dark corner of my mind, smirking his smarmy smile as he leaned against the sink while he waited for me to exit a stall. His sleezy come on. Me confused as hell. Rebuffing him, first with words, then physically, and thanking heaven and all the angels for the years of Jiu-Jitsu.

Then later, learning that I wasn't the first female cop he'd hit on, and later still, standing in a hallway in a rundown tenement in the Depot, searching for a suspect. A woman, high on a cocktail of illegal drugs. The crazed look in her eyes, her emaciated hands wrapped around the grip of a .45. Drawing my gun, the shot echoing down the long hallway, drawing the dead stares of the other residents, and wondering whether I'd hit her or she'd hit me.

I pinched the bridge of my nose, hoping to staunch the flow of memories. Not today. I couldn't deal with those now.

"I didn't want you to quit," Peterson said quietly, effectively breaking me out of the past. "You were a good cop, and I swore—"

"Fine," I said, cutting him off. I didn't want to hear some farfetched malarky about how sorry he was. It was more than I could take today. "I don't have time for this."

"No, you don't." He ran a hand over his hair, smoothing it down, then met my gaze head on. "Ammo up, kiddo. I'll drive."

I bit my tongue to keep a few choice curse words in my mouth where they belonged. "I don't need your help."

"I," he said, very carefully. "Will. Drive."

"Fine," I said again. "Whatever."

I retreated to my office, tucked my license and a credit card into my jacket, then snagged my gun and cellphone. If Peterson wanted to drive, let him. That didn't mean I trusted him.

The drive to Seth's was conducted in near total silence. Peterson wasn't a fan of ambient noise. As far as I knew, he'd never found a radio station he really liked outside of NPR and the occasional talk radio show. A big fan of stretching his intellect, he was.

I was happy reading the occasional C.J. Box novel.

About five minutes in, a message from Auntie hit my phone. I opened it and read, *Don't tempt the magic.*

That was a repeat.

I tried calling her, got the disconnected message, and, frustrated, tapped the phone to my forehead.

"What?" Peterson said.

"Nothing."

"Had to be something to get you worked up."

"I'm not—" I closed my mouth around the rest of that comment. Peterson had always been good at teasing information out of people. The tricky bastard.

My phone rang, saving me from having to finish that sentence. When I saw Seth's number, I very nearly swiped the call off without answering it. Would have if not for Nick.

I gritted my teeth and answered the call.

"Do you have him?" Seth said over the noise of a crowd of people talking.

My heart sank to my knees. Still, never assume, right? "Have who?"

"Nick."

"No. The last I saw—"

"Come to my house. Now."

The line clicked off and I dropped my phone in my lap.

"Trouble?" Peterson said.

Yeah. Sounded like there was a world of trouble brewing at Seth's house.

"Go faster," I said, then I turned my head away and stared out the window, watching the city's streetlights flash past one by one.

TWENTY-SIX

A couple dozen cars were parked in Seth's driveway when we got there. Peterson circled past the house and parked on the street, then we walked back through the light rain, using the flashlight app on my phone to guide our steps.

I hadn't brought a rain jacket because, well, I'd been more worried about Nick and the showdown with Peterson than anything. By the time we reached the house, my cloths were damp and my hair was plastered to my head. I finger combed it away from my face as we walked up the front steps.

And entered chaos.

People were everywhere, milling around the front rooms in various stages of undress, sliding between limping wolves as if they were one and the same. Many sported bruises and cuts. A few appeared to be seriously hurt.

The house itself looked like a tornado had whipped through it. Tables were overturned, pictures and paintings had fallen to the floor, glass was everywhere. Some of the spokes in the stair railing had snapped, each half little more than ragged splinters.

I caught a young woman I vaguely recognized as she jogged lightly through the foyer carrying a first aid kit.

"What happened?" I said.

"We were attacked." She jerked her head toward the kitchen. "Seth's back that way."

"Thanks."

I let her go and led Peterson through the house, goggling at the mess, then goggling some more at the size of the crowd. I'd been to Seth's for parties before, but I didn't remember there being so many pack members around for those. The sheer number of werewolves helped distract me from the frantic worry twisting around my heart.

If something could tear through an entire pack like this, what chance did my brother have?

The kitchen seemed largely intact. Maybe the fighting hadn't gotten to this part of the house. If it had, it didn't show. Seth and Miles sat alone at the table to the left of the doorway, talking quietly while Miles cleaned a cut at Seth's temple. Their conversation ended when Peterson and I walked in, and they both glanced at us, Miles wearing a rare scowl.

"What happened?" I said.

It was Seth who answered. "A rune witch kidnapped Nick."

"How do you know it was a rune witch?"

Miles' scowl deepened. "Runes. How else?"

"Pictures?" I said.

Seth shook his head, dislodging Miles' hand. "Saw them."

"Can you sketch them for me?"

Seth shrugged, which I took as a maybe with a medium sized chance of no one having seen a rune long enough to be able to replicate it. Which kinda sucked, since that left me without a way to track down the spells used and, hence, the witch who'd used them.

I worried my lower lip with my teeth. Any witch would have to be very powerful to cause this much damage to werewolves, and so many of them at once, too. Who had that kind of power? Who possessed enough arrogance to try?

My brain pieced two and two together right then. "You thought it was me. Why?"

Miles tossed the used gauze onto the table and opened another one. "We couldn't get a good look at whoever it was. They were using some kind of cloaking spell."

I almost said that I'd never heard of one, but that would've been an outright lie. I *had* heard of a cloaking spell, or something like it. One had been used to spirit Serena Jimenez away in front of a dozen eyewitnesses. One minute there, the next gone. Just like magic, only this wasn't a trick performed by a guy drawing a rabbit out of a hat for a bunch of kindergartners.

So many questions buzzed through my mind, I didn't know where to start. How many people were involved, was it all related, why had me and Nick been singled out. So many questions.

After a moment sorting through them, I settled on, "What are you doing to find my brother?"

Seth took the gauze from Miles and pressed it against a nasty looking cut on the back of his hand. "Mariah took some of the healthier wolves out to track him."

"Nick we can smell," Miles added.

"But not the witch?" I said.

Seth grunted, whether from the question or the pain of the cut, it was impossible to say. "Same problem with the other one."

"Then why did you think it was me? You know I'm not capable of this."

"Because you'd do anything to get Nick back." Seth flicked his gaze to Peterson, who'd opted to stand behind me, out of the way. "You didn't have to bring a cop."

"He showed up on his own."

Peterson jumped into the conversation then, asking questions I hadn't been able to articulate.

Fine. Whatever. Let him play the detective. I crossed my fingers together behind my nape and let my gaze go unfocused. There had to be some way to track the magic. For the life of me, I couldn't figure out what it was. Auntie O would probably know, except she'd gone ballistic when I'd tried to bring the investigation up, then done her own brand of a disappearing act.

I rolled my head back, closing my eyes against the

brightness of the overhead lights. Maybe the grimoire held an answer or two, assuming I could find someone who could read whatever languages it was written in.

Like, say, Dimitri. Strange how he dropped the grimoire into my life then disappeared. Strange how so many people kept disappearing on me.

I frowned, not out of hurt, but puzzlement. Was that really just a pattern in my life, or was something else going on, something I wasn't privy to for some reason? Like a jigsaw puzzle with half the pieces missing. You knew it formed a picture, when put together properly, but with half of it gone, you couldn't tell what the picture was. So what was the picture here? What was I missing that would tie everything together into a sensible whole? Or was I simply overthinking everything out of panic and desperation and fear?

My cellphone jangled, the ringtone just loud enough for me to hear. I pulled it out and saw Auntie O's number. Finally!

I swiped into the call as I turned my back on the quietly chatting men. "Where have you been?"

"I can't talk," Auntie O said. "Where's Nicky? I've been trying to call him. He's in terrible danger."

"I've been trying to call *you*," I hissed. "And your warning is a little too late. A rune witch just waltzed into wolf central and kidnapped Nick."

"No. No, that's not right." The words came out as sobs. "Nessie, you have to leave now. Run, darling. Go anywhere, just get away."

I felt more than heard Seth come up behind me. It was all I could do not to flinch away from his warm presence at my back.

"I can't do that with my brother missing," I said.

"You must. He's—"

A loud crash sounded from Auntie's side of the line, followed by a blood curdling scream, and then nothing.

I pulled the phone away from my ear, staring at the screen without really seeing it. "She's in trouble," I said, dazed.

"I heard." Seth walked around me and bent, putting his

craggy features at eye level with me. "Was she at home?"

"I don't know."

"I'll send a team to look."

That pulled me out of my daze. "No. Keep looking for Nicky. We need every able-bodied werewolf out searching for him. I'll go see about Auntie."

One corner of his mouth turned down. "Not alone."

"I'll take Peterson." God help me. "Call me when Mariah checks in."

He straightened and nodded, but he didn't look happy about it. "I want a text from you every ten minutes, or I'm coming after you myself."

I made a face at him, hiding my concern for both my brother and the woman who'd taken me and him in. "Yes, Daddy."

"Not your dad," he said gruffly. "But you..."

His mouth tightened into a thin line around whatever he was going to say.

I stepped away from him toward Peterson, then turned back and looked Seth straight in the eye. "Tell whoever your contact on the Council is that if something happens to my family, I'll be coming after the whole lot of them."

If he thought that was a bad idea, he didn't say so. I touched my fingers to my forehead in a mock salute and walked away. Let the big bad wolf chew on that for a while.

Peterson drove. Again. I was too wired to protest, too worn out from the worry. It took too long to get to Crossville, though he edged the Buick up over the speed limit whenever he could.

Safety first, don'tcha know.

The rain had let up by the time Peterson parked in Auntie's driveway. No light shone through the windows and the streetlamp nearest her house was dark.

The skin on the back of my neck started crawling. Peterson moved to get out, and I grabbed his forearm, halting him.

"Stay here," I whispered.

He looked at me for a few seconds, then said, "No."

"Magic. Can't you feel it?"

"Not a witch," he grumbled, but he let go of the door handle and settled into his seat. "What's the plan?"

"I go in. You stay out here where you won't get hurt."

"How about you go in and I follow about ten feet behind?"

Because I didn't trust him. Better to have him here in the car than out there abandoning me. I couldn't exactly say that without starting another round of drama, could I?

"Just let me check it out, ok?" I said instead.

He rubbed a hand over his face, then heaved a sigh. I took that as a yes and slid out of the car, leaving the door cracked rather than breaking the unnatural quiet. And it was quiet. No street noise, no insects chirping merrily. Even the wind had died down. The silence spooked me. It was like the world was holding its breath, waiting for something to happen.

I pulled my Glock out of its holster and held it at my side as I eased forward along the pathway toward Auntie's house. The gun probably wouldn't do me any good against a witch. If there was anyone inside. But it felt like there was. Felt like someone was waiting just inside the entrance.

I hunched my shoulders, easing the weird prickly sensation still tickling along my nape, and placed a hand on the doorknob. It had an odd feeling to it, a flat, dead feeling. Not that of an inanimate object. More like something had broken within it, as if some part of it had died.

Auntie's spell. But what would it have taken to break that? Unless she'd dissolved it herself.

No. That scream, the fear in her voice. Someone else had done this, someone who might still be inside.

I sucked in a breath and slowly turned the doorknob, fighting the wrongness building within me. There were protocols for things like this, steps I'd been drilled in as a cop. But those protocols had been built around humans, under the presumption that whoever was on the other side of a door held a firearm they were going to use against you.

Magic was a different ballgame. It was sneaky and mischievous and varied enough that you couldn't always guard against it regardless of your precautions. There could be a spiderweb spell on the other side of the door, designed to ensnare whatever walked into it. Or worse, slice someone into tiny pieces as they walked through it. That kind of black magic required a sacrifice, but—

My God. Had the supernaturals been kidnapped in service to a dark ritual?

I hadn't even considered it before. And I should've, would've if I'd had some goddamned help from the supernatural community on this one, witches specifically.

Too late now. I'd keep it in mind, though, assuming I wasn't walking into a trap.

Pretty sure I was.

The doorknob hit its limit, and I gently pushed the door to just past the doorframe, wincing at the squeal of unoiled hinges. A security precaution I'd talked Auntie into. An early warning system. Yet another thing designed to protect against human intruders rather than supernatural ones.

I stepped to the nonhinged side of the door and shoved the door hard enough for it to swing open under its own weight, then ducked against the house. Nothing happened. Peterson was still in his Buick, white knuckling the steering wheel.

Hey, look! The former partner had stuck around this time. Not that I counted on him staying that way.

I motioned for him to cut the headlights so I wouldn't be outlined by them when I went in. No need to paint a big, fat target on me. I peeked into the interior, saw not a blessed thing. For one, it was dark as a moonless night in there. For another... Well, I didn't have an other.

I pulled out my cellphone and tripped the flashlight app. Held it up over my head and tipped it toward the interior, then peeked in again. The living room appeared empty, but wow, was it a mess. It looked like a wave of air had burst through the door and taken everything with it, then abruptly dropped off about six feet in. Pictures, doilies, knickknacks, furniture. Nothing had survived that gush.

My guess? Whatever spell had been used to break Auntie's little electric surprise had done this. And possibly Auntie's electric spell had surged through the house when it broke and taken out all the lights. To test the latter, I reached in, felt along the wall for the light switch, and flipped it down and up.

Nothing happened, so yep, lights blown.

In for a penny, I thought, and stepped quietly across the threshold, my phone held so that the light illuminated my path. It would've been nice if Auntie had been in the living room, with or without someone holding her hostage. Preferably without, but at this point, I'd take what I could get.

I stepped gingerly through the living room, avoiding debris. A framed picture of me and Nick when we were toddlers lay face up at the edge of the debris field, the glass shattered. I glanced down the hallway leading to the bedrooms and Auntie's spell room, found it empty, and moved into the kitchen.

Auntie was sitting in the breakfast nook, her hands clasped together in front of her on the table, her hair a wild halo around her face. She looked terrified, but otherwise unharmed. When she saw me, though, she started crying and shaking her head. Her soft sobs broke the unnatural quiet, frightening me more than they should have. I'd seen Auntie cry plenty of times before. Never had I seen her look so helpless.

Glass crunched behind me. I whirled and shined the light toward where the noise had come from. A man stood in the hallway. Five ten, slender, athletic, short white hair, olive complexion. His skin was unlined, and he wore a black turtleneck tucked into slim fitting black pants and black dress shoes.

My stomach muscles tightened. The unknown supe I'd seen at Crossville Community College, Dr. Greely's colleague. Now that he was up close and personal, I remembered where else I'd seen him: A few nights ago at Kinley's. I'd waited on the bastard and hadn't even realized he was a bad guy.

My instincts had gone rusty since I'd left the force.

The man smiled at me, a genuine, friendly smile as if we were old friends. "Hello, Vanessa. Thank you for meeting me here tonight."

"Who are you?" I said.

"Christopher Penna, bounty hunter." His dark gaze flicked to Auntie and back. "Sorcerer."

A tremor of fear ran through me. Sorcerers were a genetic offspring of witches, or vice versa, depending on whom you talked to. Unlike witches, they didn't need spells to use magic; they could channel it directly from the elements, from people or objects or whatever they needed. Sorcery took years to master. They usually burned through their talent before then, which made them one of the rarer magic users.

Given their ability to channel magic at will, I bet they smelled just like chaos witches.

"You have questions," he continued. "Alas. I cannot answer them here. Be a good girl and put down the gun, then we'll go somewhere and have a nice, long chat while we wait for your mother to fetch her precious children."

I honest to God hadn't realized I was pointing my gun at him, but there it was, aimed straight at his heart. Instinct. It's a bitch.

"Tell you what," I said. "You surrender to me, then you can tell the nice cop waiting outside where you've stashed my brother and the other supernaturals you kidnapped."

"Your mother's—" Auntie yelled, then Penna snapped his fingers and she slumped lifelessly in her chair.

I sidestepped toward her, keeping my gun level and Penna well in my sights. "That was unnecessary."

"She's sleeping, Vanessa. A perfectly harmless spell. I'll teach it to you, if you like."

That earned a snort. Apparently, word hadn't gotten to him that I was a powerless little half witch. It had taken years to fine-tune the one spell I knew, and I'd never been able to perform it without the rune as an aid. For a second, I envied his nearly effortless use of magic, the abundance of natural talent and sheer determination he must possess in order to have reached such a stage.

Blowing a spell without breaking the door down? I admired that. The man himself? Not so much. Especially since he was very likely a murderer.

The question was, how was I going to take him down?

His smile gentled. "Is your arm getting tired from holding your human weapon at me? I can help you with that."

I dropped to the side, reacting more to the ping in my gut than his words. If I'd been a little quicker, I might've avoided the spell he literally shot my way by pointing his finger at me, mimicking a gun. As it was, I didn't see it coming, but boy did I feel it when it hit me. Pain swept through me so fast my back arched, then it was gone, and so was I.

TWENTY-SEVEN

I awoke fuzzy headed and irritable. The chilly air held the mineral scent of damp dirt. Something rustled nearby, then a hand touched my chin and tilted my face up.

My neck muscles screamed a protest at being moved. I ignored them and tried opening my eyes.

"That's it. Let me see those baby blues."

The voice belonged to...someone. I wrinkled my nose and tried again to open my eyes. If I could just see, everything would be clear.

"Eyes," I managed. "Not blue."

"There we are."

He sounded pleased, the voice. No, the man the voice belonged to, a man I knew, a man who...

My eyes flew open on a gasp. Christopher Penna, bounty hunter, squatted beside me, outlined by the faint glow of a lamp hung from a wire in the middle of what looked like a concrete block room. A basement?

I glanced to my left, searching for Auntie, and winced as pain shot through my muscles. "Where's...family?"

"Safe. For now."

Penna let go of my chin and stood, then swept his hand around the room. A narrow wooden table about waist high was shoved against one wall. Recesses in the concrete blocks held tools for witchcraft. A crystal ball, bottles of dried herbs and other items, books. Three large cages were set against another wall, spaced far enough apart that the occupants couldn't reach each other. The cages were just large and tall enough to hold one person each, if they were sitting.

I recognized the people caged in each one. Serena Jimenez, Billy Thomas, and the born vampire, a too thin young woman with straggly hair falling over her eyes and emaciated hands clenched tight around the cage's bars. Her eyes glittered at me from between hanks of hair, hungry and cold.

Willow. I'd almost forgotten her name.

Auntie was curled into a ball on the floor to my left, between me and Serena. Nick was to the vampire's right, his hands chained to the wall with thick, silver manacles. His head rested against the wall and his eyes were closed, but in the faint light, his chest stirred as he breathed.

I refocused on Penna, my head still foggy from whatever spell he'd shot at me. "You killed the witch. Heather."

Penna had waited patiently for me to look my fill. Now he smiled faintly at me, the expression oddly reminiscent of the smile an adult bestows upon a child who can't quite grasp a concept. "No, the vampire killed her. That's when I brought the cages in."

"Where are we?"

"You don't know? Look around and try again."

I closed my eyes against the light. Weak as it was, it still hurt. "No games, Penna. Where are we?"

"In a place where you should feel right at home."

"I hate basements."

"Ah, but where there's a basement, there's..."

It hit me then, and when it did, some of the pieces fell into place. "A house. Our old house."

"Yes. This room is where your mother performed her

darkest spells."

A laugh sputtered weakly out of me. "Mom didn't do that kind of magic."

"Are you certain, Vanessa? What do you really know of your mother's history?"

Nothing. I knew nothing, because she'd kept things from us, so many secrets. Her magic, her past, our father. We had a name and a picture and not much more. If she could keep something so important to us hidden, couldn't she just as easily hide a darker nature?

I shook the thought away and winced at the pain ricocheting through my head. No, she hadn't always been the greatest mom, but I'd never seen a truly dark side in her.

"Nasty spell," I said. "What was it?"

"Just a little something to knock you out long enough to get you and Ophelia here."

"Not the same spell you used on Auntie."

Penna laughed and his eyes crinkled at the corners. "Hardly. She's an ordinary witch. You, Vanessa, are something else entirely."

I cracked my eyelids open just enough to see him. "It's called *mostly human.*"

"Is that what they told you? Hmm."

He rocked back on his heels, then crossed the room and pulled a book from one of the recesses. Old book, thick. A moment later, he squatted beside me again, opened the book seemingly at random, and laid it on my lap.

That's when I realized that my hands and feet were free. He hadn't bothered securing me. Poor little weak half witch can't hurt a fly. If that's what he thought of me, then boy, did he have another think coming.

Penna pointed a slender finger at a rune sketched in faded sepia ink on the page in front of me. "Memorize this rune."

I squinted at it until it came into focus. The main rune looked sort of like an hourglass with the top and bottom lines crossing the upward and downward ones. Incantation symbols connected it, but not ones I was familiar with. Divination runes and spell runes were based on ancient languages and used similar forms, but there was a world of difference in both the way they were used and the way they looked.

Spell runes could be quite complex, with the base rune surrounded by symbols directing the spell toward various outcomes. My own illumination rune was one of the simpler ones: a single line similar to a lightning bolt, but with only one cross line. The incantation symbol was a tiny circle bisected by the crossing line. Anything more complex and I likely would never have been able to activate it.

I dropped my head back, letting it rest on the concrete wall, and closed my eyes again. "I can't do magic. Haven't you heard?"

"That's a lie."

"Ok, there's that one rune." What the hell. Everyone else seemed to know about it. "But it's a tiny spell. Takes a lot out of me to use it."

"Because your magic has been bound."

That got my attention. I peaked one eye open and glared at him. "Where did you get a crazy idea like that?"

"I research my marks. Do you know what magic this rune activates?"

The one on the page, I presumed. "Not a clue."

"Let's find out, shall we?"

That did not sound good. He reached for me, and I struggled to get away. Strangely enough, my limbs were sluggish, heavy. It felt as if I'd been dropped into quicksand.

"What did you do to me?" I said.

"Restraining spell. A necessary precaution, Vanessa." He picked up my left wrist, pushed my jacket and shirt up, and ran his pinky finger down the inside of my arm three or four inches, ending at the wrist joint. "Some incentive. What now, little witch?"

I stared at the blood welling up from a painless gash. He'd cut the artery. My God. My other hand moved automatically, pulling the wounded appendage close to my stomach, applying pressure to the cut.

Across the room, an eerie keening rose from the vampire's throat. The blood. She could probably smell it.

Penna peeled my right hand loose and pressed a piece of white chalk against the bloody palm. "Invoke the rune, save your life. A simple equation."

"I've never—"

I bit my lip, cutting the statement off. He didn't understand. I couldn't do magic, not like him. Never like him.

"You have," he said gently. "You just don't remember. Isn't that right, Ophelia?"

He stood and turned toward her, clearing a path between the two of us. Auntie had managed to push her upper body off the ground, though her legs were still curled at an awkward angle toward the wall.

"Leave her alone, Christopher," she croaked out. "Your issue is with Galena, not her children."

"Ah, but the path to Galena has always been through her children." Penna glanced down at me. "Quickly, now. You're going to bleed out soon."

I couldn't believe how gentle his voice was, how concerned he sounded, as if he really cared whether I lived or died. Tremors built up in my fingers, unreleased thanks to his restraining spell, and the chalk nearly slipped out of my hand. What use was it to try this spell, knowing I was going to die anyway? Should I etch the rune onto the cold concrete floor and hope I had enough strength to activate it? Didn't I owe it to myself and Nick to try?

Auntie was on her hands and knees now, her head hanging low. "Heal her, or so help me, I'll send a message spell to the Council about what you're doing here in their name."

Penna strode across the room and yanked her head up by the hair. "It won't get out. I've enveloped this room with a shield. Nothing can get in now except Galena herself."

"She won't come," Auntie panted. "She can't."

"Oh, but she can and she will."

"Do you really think she would've let you run roughshod

over her children if she had another choice?"

I lowered the chalk to the ground and inscribed the first mark, choosing to make the diagonals first. Two angles crossed, their points creating a square. Blood soaked through my shirt into my pants. I could feel the clammy fabric clinging to my skin.

Willow shook the bars, skidding the cage along the floor toward Nick. I heard Auntie gasp, but I was concentrating on the next lines, the ones along the top and bottom that would close the hourglass.

Seal the wound...

The phrase whispered through my mind as the chalk scraped along the floor. The circle was next

...make it whole.

then my bloody palm on top. My skin tingled where it met chalk and concrete. A pale pink glow emanated from between my fingers, and I felt the first stirring of magic there. More. It needed more *oomph* from me, oomph I didn't naturally possess. My skin broke out in a cold sweat. He'd cut too much, too deep. I didn't have enough talent to use a rune this powerful.

"Look at her," Auntie screeched. "There's too much resistance. She's going to die."

"Then you will lower her resistance."

"No!" Auntie said, but Penna was already dragging her across the floor toward me.

Willow's grasping hands reached through the bars, and she screamed, high and loud, then her hands disappeared, and she flung herself at the bars, rocking the cage forward.

Penna dropped Auntie next to me. Her hands scrambled over my wrist, pressing against it with one hand, plying a spell with the other as she mumbled under her breath. But her strength lay in divining the future, not healing. What could she do for such a serious wound?

"Remember," she whispered, and I glanced up from the rune. Across the room, Willow had gone into a frenzy, rocking the cage hard enough to push it to within a foot or two of where Nick lay slowly rousing himself from whatever Penna had done to him.

"Remember," Auntie said again. "I'm sorry, Nessie, but you have to remember now."

My head lolled, sagging against the wall. "What am I remembering?"

She touched a bloody thumb to my forehead. "Remember!"

Something inside me snapped, once, twice, and raw power flooded through me, soaring from my heart outward, through my limbs to the tips of my fingers and toes, bringing memories with it. Me and Nick playing in a sandbox, our hands touching. Magic sparking between us, eliciting giggles, and Mom running over, laughing at first. *No, no, don't do that.* Then the heady power of disobedience and the alarm on her expression, the fear, and strangers standing over us.

The world turned pink inside and out. I gasped and arched my back, squirming away from the pain, the discomfort, the readjustment of flesh to a magic it had forgotten, and my hand burned and prickled where it met the concrete.

Mom's voice echoed through my mind, accompanied by a faint memory of light and laughter. *Seal the wound, Nessie. Make it whole.*

And I had, and did, and would, eternally and ever, each time separate and overlapping all at once.

I heard it then, the baying of a werewolf, the crackle of chatter over a police frequency. Willow chose that moment to launch herself into the top of the cage using her powerful thigh muscles. The metal curved upward as the magic within me realigned and faded, then Willow leapt into it again, and damned if the metal didn't break.

A wand appeared in Penna's hand as if from thin air and he ran toward Willow, shouting an incantation.

Auntie's hand fell away from my forehead. "Get Nicky," she said, her voice a raspy wobble. "He's your focus. Your familiar.

Like a wand. A lightning rod."

She collapsed into a heap of dirty clothes and fragile bones beside me. Alarmed, I got my feet under me and shifted toward her, letting the grimoire slide off my legs as I moved. The bloody sleeve of my jacket rode up, exposing a vivid, pink scar along the underside of my left wrist. I'd done it, me and Auntie and...

No, just me, I realized. In the moment between Auntie touching me and her hand falling away, magic had roared to life within me and I'd healed myself.

It felt *good*. Nothing hurt, no joint pain from sitting too long, no residual sluggishness from Penna's restraining spell. No flagging energy from eking out enough magic to activate the spell, like when I used the illumination rune. I hadn't needed to concentrate or draw a focusing circle. It had simply flowed naturally. Effortlessly. To me, that was the real magic.

And the power was still there, running under my skin, in my blood. I could feel it there as I'd never felt it before, a live wire bursting to find an outlet, fierce and free. Magic and memory tangled together inextricably in my mind, magic, memory, and Nick.

Something thumped hard against wood, startling me out of my reverie, and reality plopped down around me. Auntie was hurt, a vampire was trying to uncage herself entirely too close to my brother, and two of Seth's pack likely needed medical attention.

I brushed Auntie's hair away from her face, ignoring the melee between Penna and Willow. "You ok?"

She nodded once and touched her fingers to my wrist. "Get Nicky. Broke...spell. Help soon."

Nothing about that made sense, but the first part I could probably work on. "Stay here. I'll be back."

Her eyelids fluttered closed, which did nothing to reassure me. But she was safe enough where she lay, nothing appeared to be broken, and she wasn't bleeding. That was the extent of what I could fix without magic.

Which I now had.

The thump sounded again, accompanied by the frantic howl of a werewolf, barely audible over Willow trying to break through her cage and Penna trying to stop her. Seth, probably. He'd be worried about Serena and Billy. If I knew where the basement's exit was, I'd be happy to let him in.

One problem at a time.

I checked Auntie over again. Reassured that she was probably ok, I ran to the closest cage and checked the lock.

Serena leaned weakly against the bars in the far corner, her complexion paler than it should've been. "Magical lock," she said.

"Damn," I muttered. Why couldn't my one spell have been an unlocking one or something? "Sorry. Can you change and try to break through the cage's roof like Willow did?"

She shook her head. "Not strong enough."

I glanced at Billy, who was squatting in his cage with his hands wrapped around his knees, staring mutely at us. "What about him? He's not been here as long."

"Too new."

She coughed against her forearm, and I was alarmed to spot blood on the sleeve of her shirt.

"Ok," I said. "Just hang in there, ok?"

She nodded and leaned her head against the bars, and I turned toward the commotion standing between me and my brother.

Willow had managed to wiggle her head and upper torso out of the hole she'd punched in the cage's roof before Penna started spitting spells at her. She was dressed in what had once been a white nightgown, looked like, and was now a ragged mess of dried blood and who knew what else.

Penna had stopped just out of her reach, with his wand, a slender twist of wood polished to a dark shine, pointed at the juncture of her body and the metal.

Distraction enough. I ran around him, giving the pair a wide birth, then skirted along the wall toward Nicky. He'd buried his face in the crook of his arm and was rubbing it against his shirtsleeve. Another t-shirt, this one black with the Falcons' logo splashed across it.

I knelt beside him, one eye on Penna, the other on my brother. "Hey, Nicky. How're you feeling?"

"Like storm troopers are marching through my head."

Not too bad, then, if he could joke about it, corny as the joke was. "Did you see where Penna put the key to the manacles?"

"Uh-unh." He swallowed hard and turned an unfocused gaze on me. "Can't you just pick it?"

"That was your thing, remember?"

"Oh, yeah. Magic it, then."

"I don't know a rune for that."

Though there was a grimoire laying across the room where it had fallen off my lap when I'd checked on Auntie. Did I have time to search it for the right rune?

Hell, no. It would take more time than that anyway. Find the spell, figure out how to use it, actually use it. Nope, not enough time. Penna wouldn't be distracted by Willow forever. When that wound down, what would I do? Fight a sorcerer so talented he worked as a bounty hunter for the Council?

Yeah, that was a no-win situation. He could literally put me down with a flick of his fingers, and had. What chance did I have against that? If I had my gun, it might be a different story. I couldn't feel the weight of it against my back. It had probably gotten left behind at Auntie's, so that was out. What else could I use? Was Jiu-Jitsu enough? Would half a decade of experience as a police officer, facing down the mostly not-horribly-bad guys blowing through the Crossville edition of Suburbia, be useful here?

None of that seemed like a great way to take down someone as powerful as Penna, which left me with Plan B, also known as *when times get tough, you gotta be tougher.* Since Penna had attacked me first, more than once, my nevers were safely intact due to the Rule of Self-Defense.

I was not, however, stupid enough to believe I stood a

chance against him. Penna clearly outmatched me in size, strength, power, and knowledge. He had the upper hand and he would likely break me in a hundred different ways before he tired of his little games and left my corpse to rot here while he waited for Mom to show.

She never would. Maybe other help was on the way. Peterson or Seth or, Heaven forbid, Dimitri. But until then, I was the only person here in any shape to confront the Council's bounty hunter.

With that in mind, I crept toward Penna's back, then inched forward to within five feet of him.

Then I pushed off with my legs, like a runner at the starting line, and tackled him from behind, catching him around the thighs. He fell forward, straight into Willow's arms, and I climbed up him, scrambling to grab the wand he had miraculously held onto. Willow screamed triumphantly, baring sharp canines. Her hands scraped over both of us, trying to draw us in and her head bobbed toward our throats.

Penna was too wily to be captured by a fledgling vampire still on this side of the living. He slammed his head back, missing my face by a hair, and elbowed me in the chest. The breath whooshed out of my lungs and I stumbled back, leaving him free to smack Willow in the chin with an upward thrust of his palm.

Her head snapped back, his wand hand whipped around, and nope. No way was I going to let him get another spell off, not if I could help it. I stepped forward again and thrust my heel into the back of his knee. That leg buckled, taking him down with it. I leapt onto his back, one arm around his throat, the other adding pressure to the first, and he stumbled out of Willow's reach.

"Give up now, Penna," I said, "and I'll drag you away before Willow here sinks her teeth into your worthless flesh."

He wheezed out a laugh and touched a finger to my arm. It went numb from fingers to shoulder and slid away from his throat. I fell off his back and hit the concrete hard, wobbling. He calmly turned and pointed his wand at me.

"I have a better idea," he said. "Be my student. Let me teach you how to use the magic your mother denied you for so long."

I goggled at him. "Sure! I'll just abandon everything I love and value so I can run off with a sociopathic sorcerer. Learn from the best, I always say."

He clucked his tongue. "Must we resort to sarcasm?"

"Yes, we must," I retorted, "'cause that's what I've got. You're toying with me."

"Am I?"

His answer created the first stirrings of anger, surprising me. I hadn't been angry before, not when he'd kidnapped Nick or attacked me and Auntie, not when he'd brought us here and sliced my arm open, leaving me to die. But toying with me? Yeah, that pissed me off.

My hand clenched into a fist. Boy, did I miss my gun right now.

"I wish I knew every spell in the book." Anger garbled my voice, and I didn't care. I am woman. Hear me roar. "I wish I knew them so well I could throw one at you now and take you down for good."

"You know more than you believe." Penna's eyes burned with the fervor of a true believer. "*Think*, Vanessa. Remember what your mother taught you."

"I was, what, three? How can I possibly remember anything that far back?"

"Because you have to."

He raised his wand as he said that. Some instinct sparked within me, warning me that he was about to throw something genuinely nasty at me, something I would not like living through, if I lived through it at all. Why would he use the wand when he could disable me with a simple gesture? Therefore, nasty spell.

My instinct worked that out long before it hit my brain. By then, I'd already thrown myself to the side, hit the concrete, and rolled into Nick.

Penna lifted his wand again, his expression smug and weirdly pleased. "Good girl," he murmured.

"Not a girl," I said, then I touched my brother and

remembered. Not the magic Nick and I had shared when we were little, not Mom binding our magic. No, I remembered that I *did* know a rune inside out, knew it so well that I could draw it from memory, if needed.

The page I'd ripped out of the grimoire so long ago had been a crutch, nothing more. I hadn't needed it in ages, and I didn't need it now.

My finger traced the rune's outline along the concrete as I tightened my grip on my brother's leg.

"What are you doing?" Nick murmured.

I shook my head. "You'll see." I hoped.

The tip of Penna's wand moved in lazy circles. "We don't have all day, Vanessa."

I didn't need all day. I only needed...

My finger finished the circle at the center of the illumination rune. I placed my hand over it and *willed* the magic to come alive. Power flowed through Nick into me, focusing in the hand covering the rune, and the air took on a pink glow, as if tiny lightning bugs filled the air.

"Close your eyes," I said to no one in particular, then I pushed the magic into the rune. Light and energy burst away from me in a tsunami toward Penna. His eyes went wide, then the edge of the wave hit him, knocking him off his feet. He soared through the air, riding the wave of magic as it hit Willow's cage and pushed her back, then pushed against the other cages and finally hit the wall, crushing Penna into the concrete with a sickening thump.

And on it went, radiating out of me, growing more powerful with each successive wave.

Nick's leg twitched under my hand. "You have to stop, Nessie," he yelled, but the magic was looping in on itself, feeding into him and me both. I looked at him and our eyes locked. His turned white-pink and rolled back in his head, and his body stiffened as the magic flowed between us.

This was what we had been, me and Nicky, this flesh and blood union of two souls borne of the same mother, cradled within her womb. Sharing the journey, the magic, the wonder. Sipping from the same well of knowledge, until it had been so cruelly hidden from us.

"Nessie!" Auntie screamed, startling me. My gaze swept across the room, and I reveled in the beauty, in the chaos. The narrow table had splintered, paper flew along the magic's eddies, and the metal cages were slowly being crushed against the concrete by my magic with their occupants still inside.

Serena cowered in her cage, whimpering as the bars inched toward her, and Billy gazed at me, his stare flat. Waiting to die.

The magic was killing them.

And I wielded the magic. I was killing them with it, me, Vanessa Kinley. Sister. Cop. Private investigator. I was the good guy in this, the hero.

Wasn't I?

"Let go!" Auntie yelled. Her body lay pressed against the wall, hovering three feet off the ground.

And that sight was enough to jar me out of the trinity of communion between me, Nick, and the magic.

I forced my fingers to lift away from his leg, to let go, though it felt like the hardest thing I'd ever done. I didn't want to let him go. I didn't want to lose the magic. But I had to stop or people were going to get hurt. Innocents, ordinary people just trying to live the life they'd been given, the kind of people I'd sworn to protect. The kind of people I would've given my life for when I was a cop. That part of me had never died.

My fingers popped up and I pulled away from Nick. The spell broke on a final cascade of pink light, then the air calmed and a door-shaped hole in the wall broke inward. Seth burst through it in his wolf form, with Peterson and Dimitri close behind, and I collapsed beside Nicky, nearly weeping from the loss of our connection.

TWENTY-EIGHT

Captain Jones followed the trio of males into the basement, assessed the scene, and directed the parade of uniformed personnel streaming in behind her.

Seth bounded directly to me and snuffled my knees. I sat up, careful to keep my head lower than his, and ran a hand through the soft chestnut colored fur between his ears, calming him automatically.

"They're safe now, Seth," I said softly. "You don't have to worry."

He butted his nose into my cheek, then whirled around and padded toward the cages where a firefighter attempted to cut locks using bolt cutters.

I stood slowly, surprised at the wooziness spinning my head around. Power prickled under my skin, an uncomfortable reminder of how close I'd come to losing control. Now I understood better why Auntie O had been so paranoid with her reminders. Magic wasn't a toy. And I lacked the expertise to truly wield it well.

"You'll need to get a witch in here to disenchant those locks," I told Peterson.

"I'll tell the captain." He scraped a hand over his hair, slicking the short, wet strands back. "You ok?"

"Yeah, for somebody who was kidnapped and bespelled. I'm a witch."

He cocked an eyebrow, wrinkling his forehead. "Hard to miss."

"No, I mean—"

I closed my mouth, shook my head. No idea what I'd meant or how to explain what had happened. Ten to one, the captain would want a report. Lucky for me, I wasn't a cop anymore.

"I never doubted you, you know," he said out of the blue.

I laughed. "Sure, you did. That's why you threw so many girl cop potshots at me."

"Hazing, Kinley. You were a good cop. I was trying to break you in."

My laugh died abruptly, and I glanced away. He'd broken me in, all right, so hard I'd had to quit a job I loved.

"Truman told me you came onto him."

The breath whooshed out of my lungs on a disbelieving laugh. "What? Why would I come onto a sleezy guy like Truman?"

Peterson shrugged a shoulder. He, unlike me, had had the sense to wear a raincoat. His shrug dislodged droplets of water which turned into rivulets under a second shrug. "Lady's man?"

"He's an asshole."

"Yeah. He was the one who gave me the tip in that last case, about the suspect. The one you ended up having to shoot. Said she was a snitch of his. Harmless as a fly."

"And you believed him," I said flatly.

"Until I heard your shot. Scared ten years off me." He glanced away and down, then back up again. "I shoulda told you about it beforehand, shoulda stayed behind you the whole way. But I thought, naw, she's got it. Kinley's tough, and she's trying to screw another cop, so let her handle it."

He'd been mad. I rubbed a hand over my face, realized I'd picked up the habit from him, and dropped my hand. Mad I could understand. Didn't excuse him for not having my back. I wasn't sure I'd ever be able to forgive him for that.

"How did you know my father?" I said.

"Long time ago, Kinley. Long, long time." He gestured toward Nick and the cops trying to break through his manacles. "You reckon somebody's got keys for that?"

I glanced toward where Penna's body had hit the wall. Blood and gore smeared across the concrete blocks, but Penna himself had disappeared.

"Where's the body?" I said.

"Eh," Peterson said. "What body?"

Quickly, I hit the evening's highlights, beginning with finding Auntie in her kitchen and ending with Penna being slammed into the basement wall.

Peterson glanced toward the captain, and I followed his gaze. Dimitri stood there, dressed in a sharp black suit over a royal blue shirt. He nodded once toward me, then to the captain, and walked out the door.

I had a funny feeling he was the reason Penna's body had disappeared, leaving so many questions unanswered. Why had Penna taken the witch and vampire? The werewolves' kidnappings seemed obvious: He'd planted clues at the scenes of their disappearances for me to find. But the other two? With Penna dead, we might never know.

My fault. I hadn't known what the magic would do when I cast the illumination spell, hadn't fully understood my own power.

I sighed and raked a hand over my hair, unsurprised by the rat's nest my hand encountered. "Never mind. I need to check on Auntie O."

"So that's a no on the keys, huh."

"Yeah. Sorry." Especially since a lack of keys meant Nicky might have to wait a while to get those manacles removed.

I started to turn away. Peterson's hand shot out and caught my arm, stopping me.

"What Truman did, that's on him," he said. "It's why he got

fired. But how I handled it? That's on me. I've never forgiven myself for letting you walk into that hallway alone. Don't expect you to either."

I nodded once and slipped away from Peterson's loose grip. Later I'd think about what he said, but not right now.

I checked on Nicky first, made sure he knew where I'd be, though I was careful not to touch him again. A few feet away, paramedics trained in dealing with supernaturals were trying to trank Willow. She was uncooperative. I would've found it funny except I was pretty sure that whatever had happened down here may have pushed her over the line, beyond redemption. It would've been nice if Dimitri had stuck around to help, but maybe that was too much to expect from a guy who very clearly played by a different rulebook.

Auntie had been strapped onto a stretcher by the time I reached her. I asked the EMTs helping her if I could have a moment, then took her hand and bent close, so only she could hear.

"Thank you," I said.

She turned her head away and blinked. Tears seeped out of the corners of her eyes. "I should've freed your talent a long time ago."

"Yeah, maybe. Tonight was good timing, too." I hesitated, then blurted out, "I'm sorry for dabbling with the illumination spell."

"Dabbling." The word came out on a gentle huff of laughter. "We'll work on your control."

"Are me and Nick really half witches?"

I hadn't meant to say it, hadn't even thought of it, really, but the way the magic had felt when it poured through me, the strength of it, the power. How could a half witch be capable of that?

An EMT put his hand on my arm. "Ma'am? We need to move her now."

"Sure." I kissed Auntie's forehead and told her I'd see her at the hospital, then stepped back out of their way and watched her roll out the door. Answers could come later, when she'd healed and we'd all had a chance to come to terms with the night's events. But I had so many questions now, so many more than I'd ever had about Mom and our father and our childhood.

And the magic. Always the magic.

Thinking about that bled the energy from me. I rubbed a tired hand over my nape and started across the concrete toward where Seth nipped at the firefighters trying to cut his pack members free.

That's when I remembered the grimoire Penna had retrieved from a nook in the wall and laid open in my lap. I looked around the room, searching for it, and couldn't see it anywhere. Maybe the captain or a member of her staff had picked it up, but I had the same funny feeling I'd had when Christopher Penna's body went missing, and I was pretty sure that feeling's name was Dimitri Stanislov.

It took time for the police to process the scene, time for the Council to get someone there to help with the cleanup. Captain Jones had someone take my and Nick's statements, then we were free to go home.

If she needed more answers, she knew where to find us.

Peterson ended up doing the honors, driving us to the renovated factory so we wouldn't have to call a cab. Turns out he was the one who'd called in the cavalry. Or rather, Seth had texted me that Mariah and her scent-hungry wolves had followed Nick's trail until it hit a dead end near our childhood home. Peterson had found my cellphone and seen the portion of the Seth's message allowed without knowing the passcode. He'd called Seth, and eventually they'd all winded up outside, trying to figure out how to get to us.

We hadn't needed them. Well, we had for a while, before Penna sliced my skin open and dared me to save myself. Before Auntie had released the magic within me.

Would they have reached us in time if not for the magic? I

tried not to dwell on that possibility.

Days passed. Auntie healed. Seth's werewolves reportedly settled back into their routines without too many problems. I wrapped up the case of the allegedly cheating Mrs. CFO (verdict: guilty as sin) and took on a new case for an old client. An uncomfortable distance had sprung up between me and Nick since the night in the basement. I tried not to dwell on that too much either.

Johnny Magnum, born John Timothy Rogers, was buried on a sunny October morning in the old mill cemetery on the outskirts of the depot, adjacent what would've been the historic First Baptist Church of Crossville's building if it hadn't burned to the ground.

I was surprised by the number and variety of people in attendance, everyone from Depot residents dressed in sweatpants and ragged jeans to upper crust Atlantans wearing tailored suits and dresses. A celebrity or two hid within the crowd, protected by discreet bodyguards and sunglasses.

Angel Miller was there with her children, dressed demurely in a black jacket over a black and red floral skirt. Our gazes met across the crowd gathered around the burial site. She raised her chin, daring me to say something, and when I didn't react, glanced down at her children and back to the preacher intoning a traditional Psalm over the casket.

Surprisingly, Peterson was there, too. He tilted his hat to me, and I nodded back. Maybe he hadn't been such a bad partner after all. Maybe he'd just trusted the wrong cop.

Water under the bridge. That described a lot of my life up to that point.

TWENTY-NINE

T he weekend after Penna invaded her home, Auntie invited me and Nick there for Sunday brunch. She was still wobbly. Old bones, she'd insisted, even though Nick gently reminded her that it had only been a few days since the incident.

Yeah, that's how we thought of it, the *incident*, as if minimizing that night in words could minimize the effects of it on our lives.

Nicky hadn't come within five feet of me since then, until we drove here together. It hurt so much, this distance between us, but I didn't know how to say so, didn't know how to heal a wound we hadn't been responsible for creating.

Auntie, at least, could give us answers. By unspoken consent, Nick and I waited until the meal was over before confronting her. It was the polite thing to do. Also, he'd threatened to put nightcrawlers in my tub if I prodded her before then.

Sibling love, right?

Auntie set her napkin beside her empty plate and crossed her ankles together under the table. Yesterday's wind had prefaced a storm. Gray clouds hung heavy in the sky, threatening rain. Auntie's garden had succumbed to the colder weather overnight and the trees were bare, silver skeletons. Fitting, somehow, that the world outside had changed at the same time that we had.

"There was an incident when you were younger," Auntie began.

"You mean like the *incident* from the other night?" I said.

Nicky shot me a warning look. "Tell us what happened."

"You were two, just turned. Galena had planned a wonderful birthday party for you and—" Auntie's hands came together in front of her, fingertips touching, then fell into her lap. "You must understand. The two of you always had a special bond. If one thought something, the other wasn't far behind. What one wanted, both of you demanded. There was a child."

A strange foreboding settled into the pit of my stomach. I set my own napkin aside, almost afraid now to hear the rest.

"You'd gotten a playset," Auntie said. "Galena had been teaching you runes, Nessie. I'm telling this all out of order."

I reached across the table and placed my hand on her shoulder. "Tell it in any order you like. We can sort it out." Why not? We'd been sorting out Auntie's conversations for years now.

"I had foreseen a light, you understand, though I didn't know..."

Her voice trailed off and her gaze went distant, then she recited the rest as if it hadn't happened yet. The toddler of a friend wanted to play on our playset, but Nick and I, one of us or both, didn't want to share. Mom had begun teaching me runes, a common practice among rune witches. It took years to master some, decades to master others, and so the basic forms were taught along with the alphabet.

That would've been fine with a normal witch, but I had Nicky and, they thought, we had bonded as each other's familiar in the womb. Mom hadn't realized the extent of the bonding. Everyone assumed we would naturally grow apart and find proper familiars, should we need them. But at that age, we had naturally turned to each other, and the magic had been too much for us to control.

Auntie glossed over some of the details. The toddler had not been seriously hurt. That's all she would say about him no matter how we prodded her.

Mom tried teaching us separately after that and gently discouraged us from playing with the magic together, but it hadn't worked. We'd nearly blown our nursery up one day during a temper tantrum.

Auntie didn't say so, but I was sure that one was on me. I'd always been more hotheaded than Nick.

But that had been the straw. Mom consulted the elders, a coven was formed, and our magic bound.

"She was going to release you, when you were old enough," Auntie said. "But then she..."

When she didn't continue, I leaned forward. "She did what?"

"Nothing."

Auntie shook her head, and Nick shot me another warning glance. That's the only reason I backed off, but his censure wouldn't stop me forever. Auntie knew what had happened to Mom. She owed us an explanation. Somebody did anyway and she was the only one here.

"Why didn't you tell us sooner?" Nick said, his voice far gentler than mine.

Auntie's hands fluttered around her plate and she shifted in her chair, her gaze anywhere but on us. "It never seemed like the right time. We thought it was too much for you, you see? Too much, and then I failed to teach you individually, just as Galena had, and that was that."

I leveled a flat stare at her. "So you let us believe all this time that we had no magic because it was never the right time to tell us that was a lie."

Auntie flinched away from me, but I saw the truth in her expression. With our magic bound, we'd been no threat.

There'd been no good reason not to tell us the truth. Auntie hated confrontation, though, and she hated consequences. I'd always thought those were an intrinsic outcome of being a diviner. Maybe they weren't. Maybe that was just her personality.

It was hard to be grateful in that moment. I tried to be anyway. Regardless of anything else, Auntie had taken us in when Mom abandoned us. For that, she would always have my gratitude.

I spent the afternoon catching up on chores, then put a movie on, ordered takeout, and tried to relax. My mind kept circling around to Mom and the way she'd walked out on us. No note, no warning, nothing. Then there was Penna's insistence that Mom would come after us, and Auntie's that she couldn't.

And Dimitri waltzing into our lives just before all this went down. He wasn't the catalyst, though. Mom was.

Finally, I cut the movie off and padded downstairs in my pajamas. I'd taken the grimoire Dimitri had given me to my office a few days ago and locked it in an desk drawer for safekeeping. I wanted to look at it again, but there was something else I needed to do first.

Once at my desk, I pulled out a new file folder and labeled it *Kinley, Galena*. Everything I knew about Mom went inside. The notes I'd made while searching for the missing supernaturals. A report I'd drawn up for Captain Jones' benefit on what I knew of Penna. Questions on the connections between Penna's victims and Mom, which I hadn't figured out yet. Anything I thought pertinent. Tomorrow, I'd begin looking for her in earnest. For tonight, creating the file was enough.

I unlocked my desk's file drawer, filed Mom's folder in with the rest, and pulled out the grimoire.

Then went back and added in a sketch of the runes found at the site of Seth's demolished development. Maybe they were connected, maybe they weren't. It felt right putting them there, so I did. Whether they belonged or not could be sorted out later.

Finally, I set the grimoire on top of my desk and riffled through the pages, stopping long enough to examine random pages before moving on. Some parts were older than others, as if it had been compiled from multiple books of varying ages. I couldn't read the language. It looked Latin-esque. Not my forte, but I could find a linguist or something to help me figure out what it was.

On impulse, I flipped to the very first page and discovered a list of names, the bottom one being a name belonging to someone I'd never known at all.

Mirek Novotny. My father.

The shock of seeing his name froze me in place for long moments as my mind whirred through the implications. Was this his grimoire? Did that make him a witch, or had it been given to him to keep and he'd inscribed his name inside for some unknown reason?

No, that was a stretch, a series of assumptions drawn without basis in fact.

What did I *know*?

I knew that Dimitri Stanislov, Mr. Tall, Dark, and Mysterious, had broken into my apartment one night and left the grimoire for me to find.

I knew that it was written by multiple hands, probably during different eras, in a language or languages I could not read.

I knew that it held runes of a magical nature, though what that nature was, I couldn't say.

And I knew that my father's name, or someone with the exact same combination of forename and surname, was inscribed on the very first page.

What did that tell me?

I thought about it long and hard, but for the life of me, I could draw no conclusions. It was a puzzle, just as Mom's disappearance was a puzzle.

There were more names, though, and those might also be clues. The name directly above my father's was Juri Novotny, and the one above that was also surnamed Novotny.

A family grimoire then? More research might bear out that tentative hypothesis.

There was just one problem: Everyone had led us to believe that our father was human. So what was his name doing in a grimoire which had presumably been owned or created by others sharing his name?

I shook my head and leaned back in my desk chair, intending to settle in for a long, meditative think before bedtime.

And saw Dimitri standing in the doorway between my office and the reception area.

I should've been surprised that he'd made it that far without my sensing him. Should've been scared or worried that a vampire had snuck up on me again.

But I had questions, and here was someone who very likely had answers.

Besides which, I'd gotten into a buttload of trouble because I'd broken one of my three nevers and let this guy into my life, however small a role he'd played so far. If he was going to remain in my life, and it looked like he was, since he kept popping in and out of my home, then I was going to put him to good use.

I smiled and waved at a chair, silently inviting him to sit. "You showed up just in time, Stanislov. We need to talk."

His gaze fell to the grimoire, then he smiled back, a slow grin revealing the tips of sharp, white fangs. "Yes, we do, my pet. We do indeed."

He sat down across the desk from me, and I steeled myself to play whatever game he wanted in exchange for the information he held about my family.

ABOUT

Celia Roman lives in the Southern Appalachians, surrounded by generations of family and myth. Her stories are inspired by a natural interest in the paranormal and too many late night reruns of *Supernatural*. Find her online at:

www.celiaroman.com

SUNSHINE WALKINGSTICK SERIES
Hunter
Greenwood Cove
The Deep Wood
Cemetery Hill
Witch Hollow
Devil's Branch
Vampire Alley

KAYA FOX SERIES
A Vision in Death

VANESSA KINLEY, WITCH PI SERIES
The Single Witch's Guide to Online Dating
Between a Witch and a Hard Place
A Witch and Her Familiar
Black Witch Rising
A Witch Called Justice